R0202001000

W9-AOK-027

3650 Summit Boulevard
West Palm Beach, FL 33406-4198

Praise for

Blood and Chocolate

An ALA-YALSA Top Ten Best Book
for Young Adults

An ALA-YALSA Top Ten Quick Pick

A *School Library Journal* Best Book of the Year

★ "A vivid portrayal of a young female werewolf
coming of age.... Gripping, thrilling, and original."
—*School Library Journal*, Starred

★ "Klause's imagery is magnetic and her language
fierce, rich and beautiful."   —*Booklist*, Starred

"Extrapolating brilliantly from wolf and werewolf
lore, Klause creates a ... fierce, suspenseful thriller."
—*Kirkus Reviews*

"Readers . . . will find this sometimes bloody tale
as addictive as chocolate."   —*Publishers Weekly*

Also by
ANNETTE CURTIS KLAUSE

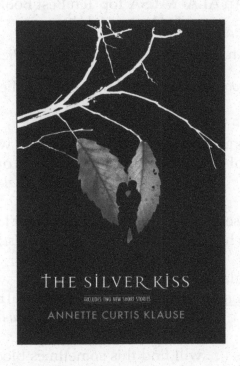

Available from Delacorte Press

ANNETTE CURTIS KLAUSE

BLOOD
AND
CHOCOLATE

EMBER

Text copyright © 1997 by Annette Curtis Klause
Cover art copyright © 2012 by Laura Clarke

Visit us on the Web! randomhouse.com/teens

Educators and librarians, for a variety of teaching tools,
visit us at randomhouse.com/teachers

The Library of Congress has cataloged the hardcover edition of this work as follows:
Klause, Annette Curtis.
Blood and chocolate / Annette Curtis Klause. — 1st ed.
p. cm.
Summary: Having fallen for a human boy, a beautiful teenage werewolf must battle both
her packmates and the fear of townspeople to decide where she belongs and with whom.
ISBN 978-0-385-32305-5 (trade) — ISBN 978-0-375-84316-7 (ebook)
[1. Werewolves—Fiction.] I. Title.
PZ7.K67815
[Fic]—dc22
96035247

ISBN 978-0-385-73421-9 (tr. pbk.)

RL: 5.5

Printed in the United States of America

First Ember Edition 2012

A book for Mummy, although I'm sure she'd
prefer cuddly, polite creatures.

Ye may kill for yourselves, and your mates, and your
   cubs as they need, and ye can;
But kill not for pleasure of killing, and *seven times never
   kill Man!*

Rudyard Kipling, "The Law of the Jungle"

In fear I hurried this way and that. I had the taste of
blood and chocolate in my mouth, the one as hateful as
the other.

Hermann Hesse, *Steppenwolf*

MAY

Ghost Moon

Flames shot high, turning the night lurid with carnival light. Sparks took the place of stars. The century-old inn was a silhouette fronting hell, as everything Vivian knew was consumed in fire.

Two figures broke from the smashed front door and ran toward the woods where she stood, their nightclothes smeared with soot, their faces white with terror. The person who pushed them out disappeared once more inside. Another window exploded.

Three of the cottages were in flames, too, and the barn. Horses screamed in terror as they were chased from the stables by a handful of teenage boys.

In the West Virginia hills, miles from the nearest town, they didn't expect a fire engine to arrive.

Somewhere behind her a woman wailed and wailed. "They did it on purpose. They burned us out."

"Get her into one of the trucks," a male voice yelled. "I'm bringing the other car around."

"Watch out for snipers," a female voice called back. "They might be waiting to pick us off as we leave."

"Head for Maryland," Vivian heard her mother say. "We'll meet at Rudy's."

Vivian felt a tug on her arm. Her mother, Esmé, stood panting beside her. "I put Aunt Persia in my car. Where's your father?" Now that she stood alone with her daughter, her voice rose high in panic.

"He went back in," Vivian answered, her words roughened by smoke and tears. "With Gabriel and Bucky."

"Ivan!" Esmé started toward the building and Vivian grabbed her and held on tight. "No! You can't both be in there. I can't stand it."

Esmé fought to get away, but at fifteen, Vivian was her match. "You can't stop him," Vivian said. "He swore to protect the pack."

"But I need to be beside him," Esmé begged. "They're my people, too."

What have I done? Vivian thought. If only she'd stopped the boys this might not have happened. If only she'd told her father they were out of control.

Figures came around the side of the house. Bucky led a slight young woman not much older than Vivian. Gabriel held a shrieking bundle in his arms.

The fire roared its victory; then, with a crack as if a giant's spine had snapped, a central beam gave way, and the roof collapsed in a peacock tail of sparks and flame.

"Daddy!" Vivian screamed.

But it was too late.

MAY/JUNE
NEXT YEAR

Midsummer Moon

1
———

"Mom, you've been fighting again."

Vivian glared at her mother.

Esmé Gandillon lolled in an easy chair, one long slim leg thrown over the arm. She refused to stop grinning. A gash in her cheek still bled slightly.

"You look awful," Vivian said.

"Yeah, but you should see the other bitch," Esmé answered. She scratched her scalp luxuriously with both hands, tousling her thick blond hair.

Vivian sighed and came over to dab at her mother's cheek with a tissue grabbed from the box on the coffee table. She would ruin her beautiful face. "Can't you and Astrid leave each other alone?" It had been like this ever since they'd moved here from West Virginia, over a year ago now. She hardly knew her mother any-more. "Can't you?" she repeated.

"Rafe called for you," Esmé said, ignoring the question.

Vivian rolled her eyes. That was all she needed. Couldn't he take a hint?

Esmé sat up and looked directly at her daughter. "I thought that's where you were, with Rafe and the others."

"No, I wasn't." She bristled at the thought. The five young males who were her only age-mates were likely to get the rest of the pack killed if they kept on going the way they were.

"So where were you?"

Vivian turned to leave the room. Since when was her mother so worried about where she was? "Down by the river, at the rocks," she said over her shoulder.

"What were you doing there?"

"Nothing."

As she left, Vivian heard her mother growl softly in frustration.

Why did Esmé always have to bring up the Five? Couldn't she get it through her head that Vivian didn't want to be with them?

The familiar knot in her gut formed hard and tight. The fire last year had been the Five's fault—and Axel's. She slammed the door of her room. The inside face of the door was channeled with claw marks. She grew her nails and ripped another row.

Axel had to go and lose it and kill that girl.

Axel had been acting wilder and wilder last spring, and talking crazy stuff. She heard him and the Five boast about midnight visits to town where they stalked humans in the shadows and scared them silly. What they did sounded funny. Vivian made them take her, too. But rumors started going around school. People were getting nervous. When Vivian said maybe they should cool it, Axel and the Five only laughed at her.

Then Axel began to go off by himself, and something seemed wrong to her. He didn't talk as much. It drove her crazy.

I was half in love with Axel, Vivian thought as she stripped off her leggings. *Rafe thought I was his girl but I would have dropped him in a second for Axel.* She sniffed in disgust. *Caring for Axel made me stupid.*

She'd seen their behavior spinning out of control, and she hadn't done a thing. She should have told her father what they'd been up to, even if that meant she'd be in trouble herself. But you didn't squeal on your friends, did you?

Then the night of the Valentine's dance Axel went to town alone and killed a girl in back of the school.

Vivian still felt the heat of anger when she thought of what he'd done. She couldn't help thinking he killed for some petty reason, like the girl turned him down. *And he could have had me,* she thought bitterly.

He must have been changing back when a classmate saw him crouched over the body. Before Axel knew he was there, the boy took off and named him to the police.

The Five decided to help. They killed another girl while Axel was in jail. They didn't let Vivian know their plans; they must have thought she'd object. *And I would have,* she thought, but she wasn't sure.

"How could a boy be covered in fur? How could a human inflict such wounds?" the family lawyer

9

pleaded for Axel. The new killing while Axel was locked up proved there was a wild animal on the loose. Axel had merely discovered the body, then had panicked and run. The case was dismissed.

But someone from town believed the witness's tale of a wolf that turned into a boy, and late one night the inn and outbuildings burst into flame in six different spots, and black acrid smoke hid the moon.

In the 1600s, her ancestors had fled from werewolf hysteria in France to the sparsely settled New World, and by the end of the century had settled in wild Louisiana. In nineteenth-century New Orleans the Verdun triplets broke the ban on human flesh and the pack moved in haste to West Virginia, where they were joined by the remnants of a German pack from Pennsylvania. Last year the forbidden appetite had won again, and the pack took flight from the hills that had been its home for one hundred years and arrived refugees in the Maryland suburbs—five families plus assorted others crammed into Uncle Rudy's run-down Victorian house in Riverview. With luck, no one would follow them here; they could mark new trails.

The house on Sion Road had emptied out gradually as the others found jobs and places to stay, until it held only Vivian, Esmé, and Uncle Rudy. Vivian had thought that by this time they would have made plans for the future, but now the whole pack seemed to be crazy, her mother included. With more than half of them dead, no one knew his or her place anymore. There was constant squabbling. Survival depended on their blending in while they organized and decided where they would move and settle for good, but at any moment the pack was likely to explode in a ball of flying fur. They needed a leader badly, but no one could agree who.

Blend in, she thought. *If only I could.*

Last summer she had hid in her room and slept mostly, and in the early hours of the morning, the time when wolf-kind come home to shed their pelts, Vivian would hear her mother crying inconsolably by her open bedroom window for someone who would never come home again.

By the time her junior year started, however, Vivian had begun eating almost regularly, and Esmé had found herself a job as a waitress at Tooley's, a local dive. Gradually it wasn't so hard to make it through the day. Vivian was no longer exhausted when she walked in the door at three-thirty, and the schoolwork began to make sense.

She started to look longingly at the groups of kids laughing together around the flagpole after school.

At first she thought, *Why would I make friends with people who would kill me if they knew what I was? What if I give myself away?* But the yearning continued. It was then she realized that she didn't know how to make friends.

She had always had the pack around her, the pack that now hid in their separate dens. There were always pack kids. She had never had to reach out for company, company was always there. The Five were still around, of course, but now she couldn't bear to be with them, and they could never be just her friends

11

now, anyway. They all saw her as a mate — be nice to one, and the others would sulk and snap. Fight, fight, fight, that's what paying attention to them meant.

I want other friends, she thought. But no one seemed to want her.

She stood in front of her closet mirror in her T-shirt and twisted this way and that. *What's wrong with me?* she wondered.

There was nothing the matter that she could see. She was tall and leggy, like her mother, with full breasts, small waist, and slim hips that curved enough to show she was female. Her skin was gently golden; it was always golden, sun or not, and her tawny hair was thick and long and wild.

So why was it that groups of girls stopped talking when she approached them at school and answered her openings with terse words that killed the conversations she tried to start? Was she too good-looking? Was that possible? Was that the threat they saw? She was a beautiful *loup-garou*, she knew — the Five howled for her — but what did human eyes perceive?

The boys nudged each other when she passed; she'd seen them out of the corner of her eye. They noticed her. And she could understand why one or two might blush and stammer if she talked to them. There were always shy boys who would die if any girl noticed them. But where were the bold ones?

Male or female, they resisted her. Could they see the forest in her eyes, the shadow of her pelt? Were her teeth too sharp? *It's hard not to be a wolf,* she thought.

12

She missed the mountain slopes where humans were far apart and the pack was close, and she hardly ever had to pretend.

I don't care, she thought, twirling around. *I don't need humans. I still have the pack, and we'll be moving on again soon.* But she did care. The pack was in shreds, and in the midst of these humans she was wolf-kind—*loup-garou*—and this made her an outsider and unwanted. *But they would like me if they took the time to know me,* she thought. *They just don't know me.*

She flung herself onto her bed and stretched her legs in the air to admire their sleek curves, holding her hips to brace herself aloft. She stretched as hard as she could, toes pointed, fingers reaching, muscles in sweet tension, almost as sweet as the change to fur. "I am strong," she whispered. "I can run with the night and catch the dawn. I can kick a hole in the sky." And she struck out with a foot to prove her words. Then curled into a ball.

She missed her father—his advice, his comfort. She bared her teeth at the familiar pain.

From where she lay, she could see the unbroken wall she'd cleared of furniture and the mural she'd started to console herself and to make this room hers.

Jagged, thick blacks made the forest a wild thing, texture on texture; the painted moon shone fiercely. There was red slashed into the dark—eyes, blood.

Loups-garoux ran through the pooled moonlight on a night in her people's ancient past. The stories said that by ritual, sacrifice, and sacrament, they opened their souls to the Forest God, the great hunter who took the shape of the wolf. To reward them for their devotion, his mate, the Moon, gave them the gift to be more than human. Then they could throw aside the pelts of hunted animals and grow their own, abandon their knives of flint and use their teeth. Their children's children's children still carried the beast within, and all were subject to the Moon.

In the center of the mural was where she would become part of the night, where she would run with the pack of her ancestors. But now whenever she picked up the brush, she couldn't go on. She couldn't see herself there. She had a dream about the painting that kept coming back. She was surrounded by darkness and she couldn't see the muzzles around her. She was running, running, trying to reach the open night, but all around the huge forms crowded close and abraded her skin with their harsh thick fur as they thudded into and jostled her. And she couldn't grow her pelt. It was always their fur against her skin, and she'd wake up crying.

As if to counteract the dream, she had become obsessed for a while and had created dozens of smaller paintings and sketches of the pack she knew while growing up. They lined her closet and were stacked in the space between her dresser and the wall. They helped her hold on to the past. They kept her from going crazy.

The art teacher thought she was one of those punk artsy types and raved about the power of expressionism.

Great Moon, he'd shit a brick if he knew my subjects were real, Vivian thought gleefully. He'd talked her into submitting a few prints to the school literary magazine. She'd laughed at first—but why not? And now, to her surprise, there was one of her prints near the center of *The Trumpet.* Vivian smiled. And no doubt those humans thought her work was the too-cool vision of the terminally hip and dangerous.

Thought of this small acceptance pushed back the gloom, and she bounded up to fetch her backpack and have another look. She should leave the magazine open on the kitchen table for Mom to see tomorrow before she went to work. Would she recognize her daughter's art? Would she be proud?

The magazine smelled glossy and was cool in her hands. She found her print and devoured the sheen of it, crisp and stark. *And will those girls at school notice me now?* she thought.

She hadn't even bothered to see who she shared space with. *Is my work better than the others'?* she wondered now. A poem was on the page opposite hers. She looked at it suspiciously. A crappy poem would lessen what she'd done, make it cheap.

The title startled her—"Wolf Change." She read on.

> Corsair of the wood
> discard your skin
> your pallid, wormlike
> vulnerability.
> Corsair of the wood

exchange your skin
for pelt of dun
and brindle luxury.

A pentagram is burning
in your eyes
and soft, pale twists
of wolfbane
squeeze your heart.
A grinding pain
is writhing in your thighs
the crunch of bones
proclaims the change's start.

Pirate of the flesh
throw back your head
and part your jowls
to sing a lunar song.
The forest paths are dark
the night is long.

She shivered in delicious shock.

He knows, she thought. *He knows what's in the picture.* Anger edged out the excitement and her eyes narrowed. Who was this Aiden Teague? Why should he know forest paths?

But she was intrigued. Maybe she should seek him out and have a look at this person who wrote of the crunch of bones, see if she approved of him.

And what if she didn't? Set the Five on him? She laughed softly, baring sharp white teeth.

2

The morning was tentatively warm, and the smell of early roses drifted over from a neighbor's yard. The day would be hot later; she was glad she'd decided to wear shorts. *Not much school left now,* Vivian thought as she walked down the tree-lined street. *What will I do in the summer?* Move, she hoped. Get out of this place.

"Hey, Viv."

A lean, muscular figure peeled out from behind a stone gatepost, and her eyes widened briefly. "Rafe," she said in casual greeting, and kept on walking. If she hadn't been daydreaming she would have sniffed him out.

Rafe fell in beside her. She noticed that he was now cultivating a goatee and mustache. He ran a hand through his thick, long brown hair and shifted his grip on a package wrapped in newspaper he carried under one arm. "Going to school?"

"Some of us do."

The Five were more likely to be found hanging

out by the diner around the corner from school, or down by the river.

"Yaaaaahhhhhh!"

"Whooooooooooooooooo!"

Two boys dropped from a roadside tree in a jingling of chains, hair flying. This time she did start slightly, and cursed herself. She should have known the others were near. The twins, Willem and Finn, looked pleased with themselves. Round-faced Willem slipped an arm around her waist and gave her a friendly squeeze. "Didn't scare you, did we?" he asked, obviously hoping he had.

"You are such a puppy," Vivian said, removing his arm. He'd been her favorite of the twins as they were growing up. He was sweeter and more predictable than his brother, but his affectionate gestures had lost a great deal of their innocence in the last year or so.

Finn, the gaunter twin, smiled sardonically.

She was expecting the others now, so it came as no surprise when Gregory, the twins' lanky, fair-haired cousin, stepped silently out from behind another tree and folded in with them, and Ulf hopped over a white picket fence to dance his jittery way backward up the sidewalk, laughing wildly, until Rafe cuffed him to the rear.

They wore their usual uniform of boots, black jeans, T-shirts, and assorted tattoos. Rafe had his sleeves rolled up to show off his biceps. *My bodyguards,* Vivian thought.

"Saw your mother go into Tooley's bar with Gabriel

18

last night," Finn said. "She was all over him." His lips sketched a spiteful thin leer, and his eyes narrowed expectantly.

Vivian bristled, but she wasn't going to say anything.

"Yeah, Astrid wasn't far behind," said Rafe. "And she looked pissed." He laughed.

"Hey, leave my mom out of it," Ulf piped up.

So that's who they were fighting over, Vivian thought. *Gabriel.* That was disgusting. He was only twenty-four. And full of himself, from what she could tell.

Rafe took the parcel he carried out from beneath his arm, and Vivian heard Ulf giggle. Rafe pulled at the knotted string to loosen it. His eyes were more red than brown when he glanced up at her, a wicked grin playing about his lips, and Vivian knew he was up to mischief.

"Vivian, I'd like to give you my heart," Rafe said, suddenly serious, then immediately grinning again. "But since that might be inconvenient, I've brought you someone else's."

The newspaper unrolled, and he slapped a brown slimy gob down on the sidewalk.

"Rafe!" She looked around wildly, hoping no neighbors were in sight. "What the hell are you up to?"

The Five were helpless with laughter.

Vivian grabbed the newspaper from Rafe's hand and scooped up the mess.

"Give you my heart . . . ," he gasped, and bent over laughing again.

Where could she put this? Where was the body?

19

She started to rewrap the disgusting trophy. Then, "Rafe, you jerk," she cried. "This is a sheep's heart."

More howls of laughter exploded from the Five.

She didn't know whether to be angry or relieved. "You were over at Uncle Rudy's store, weren't you?" Rudy was a meat cutter at Safeway. When no one answered her, she growled and flung the whole package in Rafe's face. That set the others off even worse. Ulf had tears in his eyes.

She turned and left them, but they followed at a distance anyway, and she heard their bursts of laughter all the way to school.

Mom thinks the Five have learned their lesson, Vivian thought. "Hah!" she said out loud.

When Axel had come home from jail, her father had passed judgment swiftly. The punishment for endangering the pack was death.

Vivian couldn't save Axel, but she pleaded with her father for the Five. They were just kids like her. They had only killed to prove the witness wrong and protect the secret of the pack. They wouldn't do it again. So Ivan Gandillon made them beg forgiveness of the Moon and run the Trial of the Fang down a narrow path lined with the pack in their fur, and all could take their bites. Some said that he let the Five off too lightly, although they licked their wounds for weeks. Maybe those people were right. Vivian hadn't quite trusted the Five ever since.

It wasn't until almost lunchtime that Vivian remembered that she wanted to track down Aiden Teague.

Yeah, why don't I have a look at this poet, she told herself. *See if I like him writing about things he shouldn't know about.* That was better than sitting around being miserable. Where should she look? She decided to ask her art teacher. He was one of the advisers to *The Trumpet.*

"Oh, yeah. He's a junior," Mr. Antony said, shaking some brushes out over the art-room sink.

"How would I find him?" Vivian asked.

"Well, if you hang around for another half an hour until second lunch, all you'll have to do is look out that window. He hangs out with his friends in the quadrangle, under those arches over there." He pointed with the brushes to a section of the covered walkway that ran around the perimeter of the square courtyard.

"What does he look like?"

"Oh, I dunno. He's tall, bohemian."

Whatever that means, she thought.

Mr. Antony must have noticed her blank look. "You know, a throwback to the sixties, jeans and beads, an MTV hippie."

The way he said that made her suspect that he thought he'd been the real thing at one time.

"Oh, I know," the teacher added. "He was wearing this flowery shirt this morning—lots of yellow and blue. It made me smile. Listen, I've got to grab a sandwich. Close the door when you leave."

"Sure."

Luckily she'd brought her lunch with her. She relaxed on the warm windowsill and chewed on a piece of steak while she waited. Groups of kids were scattered across the quad, eating, talking, and sunbathing. Some of the boys had their shirts off, their flesh golden and slick as if they'd swallowed the sun. They were sweet to look upon. Her eyes lingered on them tenderly as she bit into her meat.

At the next bell, the shift changed. Kids reluctantly scooped up T-shirts, soda cans, and books, and hurried to class, while others hardly distinguishable from them took their places.

I'll be late to French, Vivian thought. It didn't matter, the teacher loved her. She had a perfect accent. Vivian sat upright, and her hands kneaded her empty lunch bag. She kept her eye on the arches.

Two young men walked into view. One had dark, shoulder-length hair and wore a flowered shirt. That must be him. Another boy joined them, then a girl. They stood laughing under the canopy, the shadows hiding their faces.

So that's you, Poet Boy, Vivian thought, but she couldn't see him clearly. She wanted a closer look.

Why am I bothering? she asked herself as she went through the side door. *Because I'm a pirate of the night and I want to see who's trespassing in my territory*, she answered. But maybe he was one of her kind from some other pack. *Or maybe he just knows too much*, she thought. She laughed aloud at her melodramatic thoughts as she crossed the grass, and a spotty tenth-grader eyed her curiously. The sun was hot, so she peeled off her shirt to reveal the tank top underneath.

Shall I only have a look, or will I say something? she wondered. *"Ooooh I loved your poem."* Instantly she felt

22

like playing wicked games. She put a sway in her walk. *Maybe I'll make* him *look.*

The boy to Aiden's left noticed her first. He was a burly blond with a good-natured face and eyes that glazed over slightly at her approach. Vivian couldn't resist, she winked, and his cheeks turned pink. It was so easy. The other kid, wearing some kind of funny lopsided haircut, kept on yakking away, but the girl looked over and wrinkled her nose. She was small, with close-cropped dark hair—the sort of girl that wore black stockings even on days like these. *I'll put a few more runs in those tights, honey, if you look at me like that again,* Vivian promised silently.

Then Aiden Teague turned around to see what had captured his friends' attention. The crystal stud in his left ear reflected the sun in a burst of rainbow, and his slow easy smile sent a shock through her.

She was staring, she knew, but his face was delicious. His eyes were amused and dreamy, as if observing life from the outside and finding it vaguely funny. He seemed languid, not intense like the Five— those jangly, nervy, twitching, squirming, fighting, snapping, sharp-edged creatures who demanded so much from her. She noticed his tall dancer's frame and his long-fingered hands, and the thought crossed her mind that she would enjoy him touching her.

"Do I know you?" he asked. He waited expectantly, a bemused look on his face.

3

Vivian said the first thing that came into her head. "Um. I liked your poem in *The Trumpet*." *I don't believe that stupid sentence came out of my mouth,* she thought.

"Hey, thanks," Aiden said. He still looked puzzled.

He's not a werewolf, she thought in dismay. *How can I react this way when he's not one of us?* His smell of sweet perspiration and soap was purely human. *Get a grip, girl,* Vivian told herself. She didn't like this off-balance feeling. She put a hand on her hip and dared his dark eyes to try and drown her now. "Your poem was facing a print of mine. I was glad I wasn't next to some trash."

The blond kid brayed with laughter.

"Shut up, Quince," Aiden said, but he grinned.

"That was like some forest scene, wasn't it?" the kid with the funny haircut said. "Spooky, man."

The dark-haired girl put a hand on Aiden's arm. "Bingo's waiting for us."

"Hold on, Kelly." Aiden gently disengaged his arm, and the girl frowned sulkily. "Cool picture," he said to Vivian. "It's like you read my mind."

"That's what I thought about your palm," Vivian answered. Her response to him was disturbing but she wanted to explore it. She took his hand and turned it up, then ran her nails down the length of his fingers. He didn't resist.

"What are you going to do, tell my fortune?" Aiden asked.

"Yes," she answered. She slid a felt pen from her purse. Then, while he watched mesmerized, she wrote her phone number in his palm. On a whim she outlined it with a five-pointed star.

"What's that?" Quince said. "You Jewish or something?"

"Nah," said Aiden softly. "That's a pentagram."

"So she's a witch," Kelly snapped.

No, my dear, Vivian thought. *You don't watch enough late-night movies. The person who sees a pentagram in his palm becomes a werewolf's victim.*

"Are you a witch?" Aiden asked, his eyes twinkling.

Her voice was husky. "Why don't you find out?" She folded his hand around the sign that made him hers. Inside, her heart was thumping crazily in response to her charade, but she refused to lose her nerve.

As she walked away she heard Kelly raise her voice, but she didn't bother listening. Was that his girlfriend then? He could do better. Much better.

All afternoon her thoughts returned to him like a song she couldn't get out of her head. After a while it became annoying. *What am I, a pervert?* she asked herself. He was human, for Moon's sake — half a person.

25

It's only a *me*, she told herself, *to see if I can snare* *him*. But she wanted to know what was in a human had to make him write that poem, and she wanted to know why he'd stolen the breath from her lips.

As she reached home the front door opened. Gabriel, the inspiration for her mother's latest fight, was leaving. He filled the door frame, blocking her way. His T-shirt clung to his wide chest.

"Hi, Viv," he said. "Lookin' good." His voice rumbled like lazy thunder.

The teasing in his blue eyes made her want to spit. "Save that for Esmé."

Gabriel rubbed his chin and grinned. She noticed the puckered white scar tissue on the back of his right hand. The tip of another scar showed at his throat. "We don't see you down at Tooley's," he said, ignoring her anger.

She glared up at him. "I'm too young to drink."

He looked her over, taking his time. Before she could help it she tugged at the hemline of her shorts. Her shirt felt too tight. She was aware of a droplet of sweat that tickled its way down between her breasts. "Could have fooled me," he finally said.

She stared him in the eye, challenging him; she was out of her depth, but defiant anyway, willing her lip not to tremble. There was silence for a moment and she couldn't read his strong, chiseled face. He reached for her. She jerked back. Then he laughed like a giant and moved aside. She slid past him into the house, angry that she'd flinched, but showing him that she dared go by. She closed the door on his arrogant face.

"Mom!" she yelled shrilly.

Esmé poked her head out from the dining room.

"How long's he been here?" Vivian demanded.

"Only a few minutes," Esmé answered. She looked smug. "He dropped by to invite me for a late-night drink."

"Dammit, Mom. He's twenty-four."

"So?"

"You're almost forty."

"Well, rub it in." But nothing was wiping the smile off Esmé's face.

"Don't you think it's a little bit disgusting?"

Esmé flung her hands in the air. "Well, for goodness' sake, I'm not serious about him."

"Oh great. Now he's your boy toy."

Esmé smirked. "Some boy." She danced up the stairs, her rear end wagging like a tail. Vivian followed Esmé up and slammed the door of her room.

Rudy had gone to Tooley's bar after work, so there were just Vivian and Esmé at the dinner table. Vivian was still brooding about Gabriel's visit. She thought of her father and the aching emptiness that still gnawed at her. Her parents had seemed so happy together. She'd thought her mother shared that ache, but now Esmé was acting like a stupid fourteen-year-old.

"Didn't you love Dad?" she finally said.

Esmé looked startled at this question out of the blue. "Yes, I loved him."

"Then why are you out running around?"

"A year's a long time, Vivian. I'm tired of crying. I'm lonely. Sometimes I want a man in my bed."

Vivian grabbed her plate abruptly and headed for the kitchen. Couldn't her mother talk to her as if she was a daughter? She scraped her leftovers into the trash with a squeal of knife against porcelain.

"Watch those dishes!" her mother yelled.

That's more like it, Vivian thought.

An hour later Vivian was on her bed doing some halfhearted studying for Chemistry, when the phone rang. She picked up the phone on the second-floor hallway, expecting to hear one of the pack, but it was Aiden.

"There's a free concert at the university this weekend," he said. "Sunday afternoon. You wanna go . . . maybe?"

Her eyes half closed and she licked her lips. "Maybe. Who's playing?"

He mentioned a band she'd never heard of in reverent tones that suggested it was well known and one of his favorites. He was sharing a special treat with her. "I'll have to see if my family has anything planned," she told him. "I'll let you know tomorrow." No sense in letting him think her too eager. "No. Don't worry. I'll find you."

Vivian hung up and stretched her arms to the ceiling contentedly, arching her back. Should she go, or was having him rise to the bait good enough?

But a shadow slid across her pleasant mood. If they went on a date he would want to kiss her. Would he be safe if he came close enough to fill her nostrils with his scent?

Esmé walked out of her bedroom. She was wearing

the tight black dress she used for waitressing. "Who was that?" she asked casually as she put in an earring.

"A boy from school."

Esmé paused. "Oh?"

"He asked me to a concert."

"One of *them* asked you out?" Her mother's expression combined repulsion and surprise. "I won't allow it."

Vivian bristled. "You can't tell me who to date."

Esmé put her hands on her hips. " 'Don't date if you can't mate,' the saying goes." Human and wolf-kind were biologically incapable of breeding.

"I'm going to a concert, not having his baby," Vivian snapped. "And don't tell me wolf-kind only start relationships when they want children. I know better."

"You've got a smart mouth, girl," Esmé called as she walked off.

Now Vivian was sure she was going.

He had phoned, and she wasn't an outsider anymore—untouchable and strange, perhaps invisible. But why should she care so much? He *was* a human after all: a meat-boy scantily furred, an incomplete creature who had only one form.

How sad, she thought, and suddenly she craved the change.

Like all her people, at the full moon she had to change whether she wanted to or not, the urge was too strong to refuse. Other times she could change at will, either partway or fully. Right now the moon swelled like a seven-month belly, and she wanted to change because it was possible. She wanted to run for the joy of it.

29

She stalked through the backyard dusk, across the bat-grazed clearing in the narrow ribbon of woods out back, over the stream, up the embankment, and down into the wide grassy valley that held the river.

The grass was already high. Here and there might be nests made by kids making out or getting high, but she sniffed the air and smelled no human flesh.

Down by the river was a giant tumble of rocks that screened the riverbank. Behind the rocks, amid the shoulder-high weeds, she slowly slid off her clothes. Already her skin prickled with the sprouting pelt. A trickle of breeze curled around her buttocks, and her nipples tightened in the cool air off the river. She laughed and threw her panties down.

Her laugh turned to a moan at the first ripple in her bones. She tensed her thighs and abdomen to will the change on, and clutched the night air like a lover as her fingers lengthened and her nails sprouted. Her blood churned with heat like desire. *The night,* she thought, *the sweet night.* The exciting smells of rabbit, damp earth, and urine drenched the air.

The flesh of her arms bubbled and her legs buckled to a new shape. She doubled over as the muscles of her abdomen went into a brief spasm, then grimaced as her teeth sharpened and her jaw extended. She felt the momentary pain of the spine's crunch and then the sweet release.

She was a creature much larger and stronger than any natural wolf. Her toes and legs were too long, her ears too big, and her eyes held fire. *Wolf* was only a convenient term they had adopted. Those who preferred science to myth said they descended from something older — some early mammal that had absorbed protean matter brought to Earth by a meteorite.

Vivian stretched and pawed at the ground, she sniffed the glorious air. She felt as if her tail could sweep the stars from the sky.

I will howl for you, human boy, she thought. *I will hunt you in my girl skin but I'll celebrate as wolf.*

And she ran the length of the river to the edge of the city slums and back, under the hopeful early-summer moon.

4

By eight o'clock the large parlor of Vivian's home was full. The pack spread around the room on couches, chairs, and the floor in a rough semicircle that faced the fireplace — except Astrid, who lounged apart on the seat set into the bay window at the front of the house, and the Five, who loitered to the side of the window, bantering and exchanging playful blows.

Among the crowd were strays who had gravitated to the pack when it came to the suburbs, and others Vivian didn't know well who had worked at the inn when she was much younger. Many of those who had gone to join relatives when the trouble started hadn't come back.

Vivian felt a pang of loneliness. *This is all that's left of us,* she thought. *And no one I feel close to. Not even Mom anymore.* She curled up smaller in her armchair.

Astrid laughed at the boys' antics. When she tossed her head, her red hair flamed against the green curtains.

With her sharp features and plump rear, she reminded Vivian more of a fox than a wolf.

Gabriel paced restlessly in front of the fireplace. Astrid glanced over at him repeatedly until she finally caught his eye; then she winked. His grin was slow and smoldering; she sat back with a satisfied smirk.

Vivian's mother saw the exchange, too. "Bitch," she muttered. She leaned across Vivian to complain to Renata Wagner, then looked over at Gabriel and licked her lips pointedly.

Renata laughed. "Stop it, Esmé."

Vivian turned away, embarrassed.

"Can we have quiet, please," Rudy shouted.

Jenny Garnier flinched and clutched her baby closer to her. She'd been as raw as a trapped rabbit since she'd lost her husband in the fire. Rudy reached out from his perch on the overstuffed arm of the couch to pat her shoulder reassuringly.

Everyone looked his way expectantly. Well, almost everyone.

Willem and Finn cackled and batted at each other to either side of Ulf, who dodged between them, a panicked look on his small, pale face. Rafe was telling the awestruck Gregory how big some girl's breasts were.

Rafe's father, Lucien, twisted around in the easy chair he slouched in. "Quit it," he growled, and raised a fist. Rafe glared at his father, but he waited until Lucien turned away before he gave him the finger.

"The insurance money's come through," Rudy said

into the silence. There was a brief hiss of whispers. "We've got enough to do what we want now."

Vivian bit back a yelp of outrage. This was the news they'd been waiting for and Rudy hadn't told her. They had eaten breakfast together, for Moon's sake.

"And the funny thing is," Rudy continued, "we wouldn't have got the money if Sheriff Wilson hadn't spent so much effort covering up the evidence that the fire was arson so his buddies wouldn't get in trouble."

"Three cheers for Sheriff Wilson," Bucky Dideron called, to gales of laughter.

Rudy raised his arms. "Okay, okay."

The room quieted.

"My agents checked out some viable properties," Rudy said. "It's time to choose where the pack will go."

"And who'll lead us," Gabriel said. Vivian was irritated to see Esmé smiling. There was no mystery about who she supported.

On the floor in front of their oblivious mother, Gabriel's sisters—disturbingly similar eight-year-old triplets—were intent on finding out who could sit on top of the others the longest. Vivian itched to go over and smack them till they yelped. Before she gave in to the itch Gabriel leaned over and whispered something to them and they settled down.

Old Orlando Griffin spoke up in a quavering voice. "Rudy, you're the one who's pulled it all together. You took us in when we were homeless, helped us settle in an unfamiliar place, found the lawyers, and found the agents. You've been a good leader while we've been here." He pointed to Rudy with a burn-scarred hand. "I vote you leader for the move."

"I appreciate your support," Rudy said. "But I'm not going with you."

"Rudy!" Esmé exclaimed.

Rudy ran his fingers through his badger-gray hair. "My life's here. I was willing to help while I could and get things going again, but now it's time for you to move on, and for that you need a different type of leader than I have the strength or the will to be."

"You're assuming a lot," Astrid called from her window perch.

Rudy's brow creased. "What do you mean?"

"What if we don't want to go?"

Vivian was amazed when Astrid wasn't immediately shouted down.

"You've got to go," Rudy said. "This isn't the place for the pack. There are too many humans, too close together. With this many of us, sooner or later someone's going to make a mistake, and this time it might mean the end of us. Look at those boys." He pointed to the Five. "Don't tell me they've got the common sense to stay out of trouble."

"They're only being boys," Astrid said, smiling indulgently at the Five.

"And maybe they got a point," Lucien Dafoe said. "Maybe it's time to change the rules. Maybe it's time to hunt instead of be hunted. That's my opinion."

"We know about your opinions," snapped Aunt Persia, the elderly healer.

And your drinking, Vivian thought. He hadn't handled his losses well. If anyone was a menace, he was. What if he lost control and revealed himself in some bar one night? Rudy was right. They had to get out of the city.

"But we've only now settled in," Raul Wagner said. "We've got jobs." He nodded toward his wife, Magda. "We've finally got a decent house."

"And look what's happening to our kids while we're busting our asses trying to earn enough to live in this city," his brother, Rolf, answered. "We need to live somewhere where we can afford our own business again, where we can make our own hours, make time for the kids."

"Mom," Vivian whispered anxiously. "What do you want?"

Esmé shook her head. "I like it here." But she looked unsure.

I always took it for granted that everyone agreed, Vivian thought. *That when the time came we would go.*

The Wagners were arguing among themselves now, as if no one else existed; the triplets were wrestling and squealing again; Orlando Griffin was trying to raise his voice above the racket. Jenny Garnier burst into tears and the baby joined her.

Rudy jumped up. "Shut up, all of you!"

His words didn't do any good. The noise crescendoed. Vivian put her hands over her ears and wished they'd go away. She saw the Five edging toward the door.

Then Gabriel strode across the room and leaped onto the coffee table. "Quiet!"

The Five froze. The room fell silent. Almost.

Rudy knelt beside Jenny to comfort her, and gradually mother and baby stopped sobbing.

"A strong leader has control, Rudy," Astrid said. "Maybe the reason the boys are running a little wild is you, not the city. I think with the right leader we can make a good life here." She studied Gabriel with pleasure. "I know a good strong man when I see him."

"You've known a lot of them," Esmé said loudly.

Astrid's lip twitched but she suppressed the snarl. "What do you say, Gabe? Want to stay in town and lead the pack?"

Gabriel looked from one of the women to the other with languid amusement and Vivian thought she'd die of shame.

"Yes, *Gabe*," Esmé said sweetly. "You've been very quiet. What do you say?"

"I vote we go," Gabriel said, and jumped down from the table.

Astrid stared at him in amazement.

"Hah, I vote we go, too," cried Esmé, "with Gabriel to lead us."

Raul stepped forward to face Gabriel across the coffee table. "What makes you a leader, puppy? I've got years on you."

Several other males stood up to argue their cases.

"Come on, let's vote on this," Rolf said. "Let's be fair."

"Who said this was a democracy?" cried Lucien.

"It's not," said Aunt Persia, in a voice that rang effortlessly above the others, startling them all. The keeper of ancient magics raised her hands slowly, her rings glittering. "It is time," she said, "to choose a leader in the Old Way."

"But that's like stepping back into the Dark Ages," Esmé cried into the shocked silence.

Vivian was stunned. The Old Way? When was the last time they had done that? Yes, her father could have taken on any male around and come out on top, but he had been made leader because of his management skills, and no one had challenged that. He was respected and well loved.

"Not completely the Old Way," Astrid said. "Times are different."

Aunt Persia eyed her coldly. "Males only."

"No!" Astrid pounded her seat with a fist.

"You want to get us all arrested?" Renata asked.

"There are several state parks in driving distance," Gabriel answered. "Places that are deserted at night."

"We've lost so many of us," Rudy said. "Do we want to cause death and injury to those who remain?"

"A leader must have the support of all the pack," said Aunt Persia. "If there is no agreement, then the right must be won by combat."

"The Old Way, the Old Way, the Old Way," the Five began to chant. Rafe grinned gleefully; Finn's eyes sparkled as bright as the chains around his wrists.

Orlando Griffin rose and walked to the center of the room. The noise subsided. "As oldest male, I preside in matters of Ordeal," he said. He pointed at the Five. "You are not of age. We do not wipe out our young."

"We can fight," Rafe snarled.

Whatever the other boys said was drowned out by the crowd. Everyone had an opinion. Everyone expressed it.

Vivian got up quietly and slipped out the door. No one noticed. No one stopped her, not even her mother. It was a relief to leave the house.

Outside, she sat on a bench under the ramshackle grape arbor, half hidden by the trailing vines. The backyard was quiet except for the chirping of tiny nightlife. Early fireflies danced in the shadows.

She had never witnessed the Ordeal. All she knew was that every adult male fought in his wolf-shape until one was left standing—the strongest, the smartest, sometimes the most devious.

She felt a surge of exciting heat, thinking of them in a tangle of fur and limbs. She pictured Gabriel, half changed, his scarred chest glistening with sweat. She shrugged the image off in anger. Would he win? And would her mother make a bigger fool of herself to become his mate and be Queen Bitch again?

The screen door slammed.

The Five came out into the back, mumbling and growling.

"That worn-out old dog," Rafe said. "He can't tell us we can't fight."

"Damn right," agreed Gregory. "We deserve a chance."

Vivian laughed.

The Five converged on her. They peered through the vines like angry satyrs.

Rafe tore aside the tangle of stems, and his claws grew. "What's so funny, Viv?"

"You," she said. "You honestly think you'd have a chance in the Ordeal? That the pack would follow you? Grow up."

Rafe bared his teeth. His new beard gave him a demonic look. "The fight's the thing," he said tightly, but she knew his fantasy was to win.

"I don't want to get dragged back to the sticks again," Willem said, almost pouting. His twin gave him a glance of disgust.

"Why not?" Vivian asked. "Life was good there. The hunting in the hills, long runs with no one around, no one to cry wolf, no hiding, no skulking, no worrying."

"No fun," ended Rafe.

"I don't like your kind of fun," she said. "It doesn't amuse me to rouse lovers out of the long grass by snapping at their heels, or to creep up on children at dusk with my fur on to hear them scream."

"It's a laugh, Vivian," Gregory said. "Just a laugh."

"You used to think it was funny," Willem said, looking hurt.

"And how funny will it be when you scare the wrong person and get a bullet in the face?" she asked. "You might be stronger than *Homo sapiens*, you might heal faster, but you're not immortal. You *can* die if your head's blown off. It's not only silver bullets or fire that kills us; anything that severs the spine will do."

"Come on, Viv. Don't worry," Willem said gently. "We'd get them first, honest."

Vivian groaned and a cold thread of fear ran through her. "That's exactly what I *am* worried about. This is the same shit that got our home burned and my father killed."

Rafe swung himself through the crumbling frame of the arbor. Moonlight lent a brief sheen to his sleek, muscled arms. "But it's different in the city. Better. Lots of people. Lots of suspects. Easy to hide."

"Anonymous," Gregory agreed, shredding leaves from the length of a stem.

"Don't act so prissy, Viv," said Finn. "You've got a taste for boy flesh, they tell me." He ran a tongue over teeth that were pointier than they had been seconds before.

"Who told you that?" she snapped.

"Mom said you have a date tomorrow," Gregory answered with a sly smile.

Blast Esmé; she'd told Renata. "So what?" Vivian said. "I'm going to a concert, not disemboweling him. I don't think that's going to get anyone into trouble."

Rafe stepped closer. "We don't like our woman hanging out with meat-boys. It's unnatural." His breath was hot on her face. "You better not choose some meat-boy over one of us."

"Piss off," Vivian spat, and got up. "No one tells me what to do." She shoved Rafe away so she could pass him, catching him off guard.

"You're not Princess Wolf now," Rafe growled behind her. "Wait too long and we'll take what we want."

"Don't give that human anything we can't have," Finn called after her, "or we'll give him something, too."

As she stalked into the house, Vivian heard Ulf's high-pitched giggle.

Damn them, she thought.

5

"You're not wearing that dress, are you?" Esmé demanded.

Vivian looked down at the slinky tank dress that sheathed her. "Yeah. Why not?"

"Don't you think it's a bit small?"

"It's supposed to fit like this." The soft yellow dress clung to every curve as she crossed the dining room. Vivian smiled wickedly at the fleeting glimpse of her leggy reflection in the glass front of the curio cabinet. "Anyhow, it's hot out."

"It damn well will be, with you wearing that," Esmé said. "I don't want you giving that boy ideas—not a meat-boy."

"And you never give anyone ideas, do you?" Vivian answered.

Esmé looked as if she was about to grow claws but instead she asked, "Where did you get that ridiculous dress?"

"Your closet, Mom." Vivian grabbed her tiny best purse from the hall table. "I'm waiting outside."

She swept out the door and slammed it behind her. She imagined with pleasure her mother inside, fuming. Esmé wouldn't follow her, Vivian knew. She'd pretend that Vivian hadn't bothered her in the least.

Vivian waited on the sidewalk at the edge of the lawn. What if he'd changed his mind? What if he'd decided he didn't want to go out with her after all? She glanced down the road. What did he drive?

A blue sports car tore down the street, speakers blaring nightmare tom-toms at a thousand decibels. It didn't stop. Well, that figured. She couldn't see Aiden Teague in a Corvette, somehow.

Two other cars came down the road in the next seven minutes, and each time her breath caught in her throat, but each time they drove on by.

She began to have second thoughts. *What if I can't act normal with one of them? What if he tries to kiss me and I bite him?* But she couldn't go back in the house and face Esmé's smug looks.

Finally, an oddity made a left turn from Madison and chugged along the street, a giant yellow bug that squeaked to a halt in front of her house. Aiden removed his sunglasses and smiled lazily out the window at her. She consumed the beauty of him. He sported another outrageous shirt and looked rumpled and warm, as if he had just woken up. The thought of him in bed made her flesh heat and her fears dissolve.

"Like it?" he asked, patting the side of the car.

"Like it?" she said. "I'm not even sure what it is."

"Volkswagen Beetle," he answered. "Circa 1972. It sends my father right up the wall—not only is it imported, but it's the sort of car 'those damn hippies' used to drive."

She nodded in sympathy. "I like the dragon on the door," she said.

"Yeah, Jem did it for me." His eyes widened. "Hey, maybe you could paint something, too. You're an artist."

She stroked her lower lip and watched him watching her do it. "Maybe."

He grinned. "Hop in, we'll be late."

The curtain on her front door window dropped when she looked over. *Nosy, nosy,* she thought smirking, and walked casually around the front of the car to the passenger side.

The car smelled of banana and old plastic. There was a book called *Witchcraft for Tomorrow* on the floor. The seat groaned as it swallowed her, and her dress rode high. She wondered how she would ever get out gracefully when the time came. The look on Aiden's face as he gazed dreamily at her legs made her realize he hoped she didn't figure out how. *Touch me,* she thought.

"Are we leaving?" she asked, smoothing her hands down her thighs.

He blinked and paid attention to the wheel once more. "We've got to pick up Quince," he said as he ground the gears and the car jerked away from the curb. He cranked up the radio and she relaxed, happy to enjoy the sweet sweat of him, the light fur of his legs, and the way he flashed her smiles like heat lightning.

Quince lived in a brick rambler near the university. Vivian had to get out so he could jam himself past the folded-down seat and into the back. She swallowed a chuckle when he actually blushed at her leggy exit, but she wished she didn't have to share Aiden with him. She listened to Aiden and Quince yelling back and forth above the rumble of the engine and the roar of the music—who was going to the concert, who wouldn't be there—and tried to picture what was in store for her this afternoon.

The parking lots at the university were packed. Aiden finally parked on a field that had been roped off into temporary aisles. He took her hand, pretending to be casual, although she could smell in his sweat that he wasn't calm; then they followed the noise of the warm-up band until they found the outdoor arena. They wound their way around the patchwork of body-strewn, multicolored blankets laid on a gently sloping lawn, down to a semicircle of tiered stone seats that faced a stage laden with a confusing melodrama of scaffolding, wires, lights, and amps.

"There's Kelly," Quince yelled over the music, pointing to their left. "Keh-LEY!" he boomed, waving his arms above his head.

The small, dark-haired girl who'd been with Aiden at school waved back, and two other girls camped out with her on the top tier cheered. Vivian and the boys picked their way around the perimeter of the theater, trying not to step on hands or knock over bottles.

"Women!" Quince yelled, and flung himself upon

the two nameless girls, biting necks and squeezing as they exploded in giggles.

"You remember Vivian, don't you?" Aiden asked Kelly.

"Yeah," Kelly said, not bothering to look at Vivian. She wore a black T-shirt, black shorts, and low black boots. Vivian hoped she sweltered.

"Hey, man." The hipster with the lopsided haircut she'd seen with them the other day joined them. He turned out to be Jem, the dragon artist. He doled out sodas from an oversized cooler. Aiden grabbed two Cokes and collapsed onto the stone ledge, flicking his hair back. He handed Vivian one when she sat beside him. Vivian was annoyed that Kelly was on his other side talking incessantly, so she sat close, almost touching, and let him feel her breath on his neck. His head turned, his eyes questioned, and his breath mingled for a moment with hers.

"Jeez, they suck," a tall redhead said, climbing over the seat on Vivian's other side and nodding toward the stage. "Yo, Aiden." He slapped Aiden's hand.

"Go home!" his pudgy sidekick yelled at the band. Some kids behind him told him to sit down, and he made a rude gesture at them with little malice attached.

Another girl, a blonde with a nose ring and a pimple on her chin, was close behind them. "Yeah, sit down, shut up, and gimme a beer," she said.

"Christ, Bingo, you're gonna get us thrown outta here," Jem complained. Vivian didn't know if Bingo was the girl or the pudgy guy who pulled a red-and-white can from his backpack.

"Bingo!" Aiden held out his arms to the blonde, and Vivian's eyes narrowed.

The blonde leaned over and planted a fat, sisterly kiss on his forehead. "Hiya, douchebag."

Vivian relaxed.

Bingo noticed Vivian. "Hey, new girl."

Vivian raised two fingers in acknowledgment and said, "Hi." That was good enough for the blonde; she climbed into the row in front and went back to teasing Pudgy Boy.

A crashing chord filled the air, and the band onstage filed off. Some in the crowd applauded, a few whistled, but most seemed to be of the same opinion as the red-head. "Vi-sions, Vi-sions, Vi-sions," some kids in front chanted, impatient for the next act, and others took up the call, but no new band came out. Instead, fuzzy loud rock blurted out from a nearby speaker.

"You go to Wilson?" one of the giggling girls asked.

"Yeah, she does," answered the redheaded boy. Vivian was surprised he knew.

"Who do you hang with?" the girl asked.

"No one really," Vivian answered.

"I've seen you with those hard-core types down by the park," Kelly said, a sneer in her voice.

"You mean the Five," Vivian answered, unwilling to disown them in the face of Kelly's scorn, no matter how she felt about them right now.

"Is that what they call themselves?" Kelly laughed.

"It's what my family calls them," Vivian said. "They grew up together."

"You're related to them?" Kelly asked, seeming shocked.

"They're cousins, sort of."

"Ooh, they're cute," said the other giggler. "Especially that one with the little beard."

"Stay away from him; he bites."

The girl giggled louder.

Two boys in baggy shorts, high-tops, and loud T-shirts showed up and slapped hands with the other boys. "This is Vivian," Aiden said, slinking a firm arm of ownership across her shoulders in response to their covetous gazes. Vivian's toes curled with pleasure at the pride in his voice, and she glanced Kelly's way. She liked the way Aiden made her feel like a treasure others should envy him for having. If one of the Five had acted that way she'd have been annoyed, but Aiden made it seem right.

"Welcome to the Amoeba," one of the boys said.

"The Amoeba?" she asked Aiden.

"The gang," he said, tossing his hand to indicate all around. "My people. A large amorphous mass that keeps on changing size, hasn't much apparent use, sometimes makes you sick, and occasionally breaks off into smaller parts that act exactly like the parent."

Behind her laughter Vivian inspected him with interest. He had a sense of pack. She liked that. In fact, despite Kelly, she liked his pack. They hadn't challenged her, they had accepted her. Get more than one of her people together nowadays and the sparks flew. This comfort was a relief.

Kelly stood up. "We're going to the bathroom." All the meat-girls followed her obediently; she was head bitch.

"Coming?" Bingo called over her shoulder.

Vivian shook her head. *I piss when I please,* she thought.

As Aiden bantered with his friends, Vivian teased herself with his closeness. He felt good, he smelled sexy, she didn't know why she'd worried so much before. If she bit him it would be a bite he'd enjoy. Her breast lightly touched his arm and her breath skipped faster. When would he kiss her? Would she like it? She had only kissed her own kind. Could it compare?

Right after the girls filed back from the bathroom a cheer went up from the crowd and Vivian automatically looked at the stage. Six figures in motley colors pranced out, grabbing instruments and mikes. The fuzzy loudspeakers cut off midphrase and in seconds the air was laced with live music.

The tunes were light, jangly, and airy, full of love and dreams, totally different from the thumping, grinding, wrenching music the Five played loud— music to rip out guts by, Vivian called it, though she couldn't deny that it usually gave her a fierce delight. But this music was good, too. There was a sweet yearning in it. She let the music take her, so she could be one with something for a while, instead of an outsider looking in.

The sun was warm on her back and she sucked the

warmth up like life. Aiden's hand slid across her neck. She turned to him and met his eyes.

"What red lips you have," he said in her ear.

Did she dare say it? "All the better to kiss you with, my dear," she replied.

And then their lips met.

He was gentle. She hadn't expected that. Kisses to her were a tight clutch, teeth, and tongue. His torturing hands slid down her sides and lightly caressed her back. When he flicked her lip with his tongue, she parted her mouth to invite him in. Instead, he pulled away and sighed. She was intrigued.

His eyes were shy beneath his dark lashes, and his lips curved with delight and desire—desire he wouldn't force on her. Then the crowd was on its feet, moving to the swelling music she had forgotten about, and they had to rise and be part of the world.

She looked around her at the excited faces. They were different. He was different. She realized she didn't know their rules.

Bingo danced on her seat in a swirl of shirt, the gigglers danced in the aisle, and the crowd around bobbed and waved their arms. When Aiden pulled Vivian close to sway alongside him she met his embrace, but how close was she allowed? She didn't want to scare him away but she didn't like to wait. Maybe this was all wrong.

This is the last time, she thought. *No more dates. I can't go through this agony.*

The crowd was cheering and his fingers tipped her chin. His soft lips were on hers once more, his tongue more adventurous, but his hands still tame. *It's a game,* she thought, *a game of pretend we don't want sex so badly.* Maybe he thought wanting wasn't polite.

His eyes were closed. He enjoyed her taste. His nostrils flared with the smell of her. That was good. But as her eyes began to close, too, she saw familiar figures on the hill above—the Five.

A busty girl was draped around Rafe's neck, his hand inserted halfway down the back of her shorts. Three other teased-hair dolls in jeans and skimpy tops completed their entourage. This wasn't their music— far from it; they were spying on her.

Vivian took a lesson from Pudgy Boy and made an unmistakable gesture in their direction, behind Aiden's back. Then her fingers curled in Aiden's hair. *I will teach you to be less polite,* she thought.

6

That week Vivian couldn't tell if the singing in her blood was for Aiden or for the ripening Midsummer Moon. Each night she ran for joy, but *It's not love,* she argued to herself at breakfast as she traced Aiden's face in her mind. *I'm only having fun.*

She came to school early so she would have more time with him, and they stole kisses in the hallway between classes. She liked to watch the color rise on the cheeks of the young men who passed, and see the envy on the faces of the unkissed girls. *I am someone now,* she thought.

Aiden had a job after school in a video store so she couldn't hang out with him then, but he called her in the evenings, waking her from her prerun nap, and it turned out they had a lot to talk about. He liked to play "what if." He'd say, "What if a mysterious illness wiped out everyone on Earth but us, what would we do?" and they'd make up all sorts of possibilities.

Vivian was reluctant to answer his questions about her family at first, but before long she revealed that her father had died in a fire, and that she was always fighting with her mother, although she didn't tell him what those fights were about. He never made fun of anything she cared about, and he was always interested in what she had to say. What a relief to have someone to listen to her, even if she could only talk about half her life.

Kelly stopped showing up in the quad at lunch, and she took the gigglers with her wherever it was she went. *Smart choice, girl,* Vivian thought. *'Cus one wrong move and I'll be on you.* The thought crossed her mind that maybe now she understood why Esmé fought Astrid. She shrugged that off fast. Esmé had no right to fight for Gabriel; he was too young for her.

"There's an antiprom party at Bingo's house Saturday," Aiden said one day. "Her parents are away. It'll be wild."

"I like wild," Vivian said, nuzzling his ear. Saturday maybe she'd make him hers for sure.

But on Thursday night when she flung up her bedroom window and looked at the sky, she realized that the moon would be full on Saturday. There was no way she could go to that party with Aiden. The hair prickled roughly on her arms. She climbed hastily onto the porch roof outside her window, leaped to the yard, and the change was upon her almost before she reached the cover of the riverbank weeds.

The nearer to full moon, the quicker the change, the less control; and the night Earth's sister loomed round and whole there was no choice—a *loup-garou* must change no matter what. *Saturday,* Vivian thought with

54

dismay as she shuddered to all fours. But then the perfume of the night wiped away her thoughts.

Before dawn Vivian stretched into her human shape
amid the weeds, wiping the river mud in smears across
her naked abdomen. She yawned wide, tongue curling.
Time for another nap before school.

The tall grass rustled, but there was no wind.
Vivian's eyes narrowed. Then she sniffed the musky
smell of wolf-kind and her hairs lay flat again.

"Vivian," a harsh voice whispered. Rafe crawled
from his hidden nest. He waved her underwear at her.
"I've been waiting for you."

"Gimme those." She snatched them from him.

He crouched, watching her dress. "I miss you,"
he said.

Vivian shrugged. "You see me."

"Not like before."

"We grew apart. You know." They'd been through
all that.

"I don't understand you, Vivian."

"You sound like my mother."

Rafe stuck his face in hers. "You broke up with me
because of the girl I killed to get Axel out of jail," he
said. "But I bet if you got a sniff of human blood you'd
get your muzzle wet."

She jerked away.

When the Goddess, the Lady Moon, gave wolf-kind
the gift to change, she warned the first *loups-garoux* to
pity humans for their soft, immutable flesh, for wolf-
kind had once been like them. "Use your eyes," the
Goddess said. "Look at them and praise my name for

55

changing you; kill them and kill yourselves." But humans were vulnerable and preylike. They triggered the instinct to hunt.

"We should stay far from humans when we're changed."

"They are ours to hunt," Rafe said. "Axel knew. He couldn't hold back any longer. We were losing our balls in West Virginia, Vivian."

"You can hold tight to your balls and twist," said Vivian, dragging her T-shirt over her head.

How many of the pack yearn to hunt like the Five? Vivian wondered later as she crawled into bed. *How long do we have until we are destroyed?*

The phone rang while Vivian ate breakfast with Esmé. Rudy answered it. After a short conversation he came into the kitchen. "That was the last agreement. The Ordeal is on."

"It can't be this full moon," Esmé said.

Rudy sat down at the table with them. "I know. Orlando says that by law we have to allow a full month in case others want to come from afar."

"So it's July then," Esmé said. "July thirteenth?"

"Sounds right." Rudy shook his head. "I wish it wasn't so far away, though." He finished his coffee and stood up. "Gotta get to work."

"Yeah, me too." Esmé said. "Wash up for me, babe. Okay?" She left, followed by the sounds of Vivian's protests.

"I'm grounded," Vivian told Aiden at lunchtime. The idea that someone could limit her freedom was mortifying, but the excuse was something Aiden could understand.

"Grounded?" He looked at her in amazement. "What did you do to get grounded?"

"Stayed out all night with my cousins smoking dope." She was damned if she'd pretend to be grounded for some tame reason.

He ran his fingers through his hair as he digested what she'd told him. Silently, she dared him to tell her off. Apparently he decided not to comment. "How long?"

"Until I talk my mother out of it, which is usually a week." That was a tiny bit of truth.

Aiden's dark eyes lowered in disappointment. "I guess the party tomorrow night is off, huh?"

"Yeah."

"Never mind," Aiden said, kissing her ear. "When you're sprung, we'll have our own party."

He was gullible, Vivian thought. That irked her slightly. But he had no reason to distrust her; why shouldn't he believe?

Aiden didn't have to be at work until six so Vivian allowed him to drive her home. "But you can't stay long," she told him to keep up the act. "My mother will be home soon." That was true, anyway. Esmé worked the day shift around the full moon. Biting customers didn't make for good tips.

They sat on a log at the far edge of the backyard under the broccoli-headed summer trees.

"Which is your room?" Aiden asked.

Vivian pointed to the window above the screened-in back porch, and he sighed loudly to tease her.

"I'll miss you tomorrow," Aiden said. There were crinkles at the corners of his eyes when he smiled. He was a creature of warm sun and comfort.

"What made you write about werewolves?" she asked, thinking of the dark forest in his poem.

Aiden shrugged. "I like all that stuff—witches, vampires, werewolves. It's exciting."

"Why's that?"

"I don't know. I've never thought about it. Because I want to be like them, maybe? I don't want to be like everyone else." He carefully allowed an ant to crawl from his wrist to a blade of grass.

Vivian laughed. Any one of the Five would have crushed that bug. "I don't think you'd make a good werewolf."

"Sure I would." He grabbed her hand and playfully bit her fingers. His teeth set loose tiny lightning within her.

Raucous hoots filled the woods behind them, and bodies crashed through the undergrowth. She pulled her hand away.

"What's that?" Aiden asked.

"My cousins," she answered. "Damn them." They couldn't find him here with her. Not that she couldn't handle them, but she didn't want to raise any questions she couldn't answer for Aiden. And what if he blamed them for getting her grounded? Great Moon, they'd laugh.

"I've got to go in," she said. "I promised not to hang

with them while I'm grounded. They've only come to screw around outside and piss off my mother."

"Some family," he said, and tried to kiss her.

She hated to push him away. "Go, go, go. They're trouble."

He glanced at the woods and she saw worry in his eyes, but his lips took on a stubborn hardness.

"Please, for my sake," she said, to save his pride.

He hesitated. "Well, okay. See you before you know it," he promised, and left by the side path.

Saturday evening stretched on forever, golden with sun and rich with the smell of honeysuckle.

"Come with us," Esmé begged. Most of the pack were going up to the state park to run.

"Not this time," Vivian said. She wanted to be alone. There would be fights, she knew. They would call it playing but they would be testing each other, seeing who had what it took for the Ordeal. She didn't feel like fights. She only wanted the clear smells and the crazy stars. There was a new warmth in her and she wanted to embrace the night in peace.

You are smitten, she told herself, and she stretched like a happy puppy.

Up in her room she worked on her mural. She painted herself in her skin, watching the running wolves. It didn't look right. Maybe she should show herself changing, ready to join them.

I wish I was changing clothes to go to that party, she thought, and threw her brush down.

Red dappled the sky, fireflies flickered outside her

window—little wantons looking for a night of love—
and the voices of the dusk grew loud. The fine hairs on
Vivian's back rose, eager for the change. *Wait a while,*
she told herself, *wait till it's fully dark.* But it was hard to
wait for the night at full moon.

There was muffled laughter in the yard below. What
now? A chorus of ragged voices split the air, drowning
out the insect song. "Ahwooo! Ahwooo!"

She stuck her head out the window. "Quit that
howling out there."

The howling dissolved into more laughter.

"Come out and run with us, Vivian," Willem called.
"Please, please."

"No way," Vivian called back. She climbed out onto
the roof and looked down. Finn appeared disgusted as
Willem wrung his hands theatrically. Ulf was fidgeting
as usual, hopping from one foot to the other as if he
wanted to pee. Gregory grinned glitteringly bright; his
teeth were already pointed. "Come on, Viv. We're
gonna have a great time."

Rafe beckoned with a claw. "The moon feels good
on your back, Viv."

Vivian could feel the wolf inside uncurling, but she
laughed derisively. "It's not the moon you picture on
my back. Go visit your head-banger sluts and see what
they think of you with your fur on. They probably
won't notice the difference."

Gregory's pointy grin got wider at that suggestion
and Ulf giggled. *Great Moon,* she thought.

Willem looked up with huge, disappointed eyes.
"Aw, Viv. You never come anymore. The rabbits are

60

getting sassy. One poked its tongue out at me last night."

She softened slightly. She and Willem used to have the best times rabbit hunting. "Another time, okay, Willi? But not full moon."

Rafe put his arm around Gregory's shoulders. "Come on then. That bitch is too stuck up to hang with us anymore. She prefers meat-boys. Didn't your mother tell you not to play with your food?" he yelled up at her.

Willem shot her an apologetic glance, and Gregory blew her a kiss. Finn nudged Ulf in the rear with a boot, making him squeak. When they reached the gloom of the woods she saw Rafe toss his shirt in the air and saw Finn tip forward to stand on paws.

She sat on the porch roof, allowing them plenty of time to leave. They usually ran toward the city to find mischief in the urban debris; she would run upstream through local parks and quiet neighborhoods.

A pleasant hum coursed through her. The night began to look different—the hairs on a leaf stood huge like a forest, the edges of the trees were crisp. She lay back to enjoy the stars.

Did we come from there? she wondered. *Are we an alien race that was marooned? Perhaps our transmuting power was a survival trick, and now we've forgotten that human wasn't our first form.* Perhaps belief in the Moon Goddess was only an echo of an ancient truth.

The shingles beneath her were rough and pleasing to her sensitive skin. She already felt the beginning creak of bones reforming, the pop of sinews changing.

61

She forced down the cramp in her gut; she would have to leave soon. She couldn't change on a rooftop lit by moonlight. What would the neighbors think?

As if on cue, she smelled the odor of a human. Someone taking an evening stroll, perhaps?

There was scrabbling down where the drainpipe emptied. Rat? She rose to a crouch. No, someone was climbing the pipe. She heard a muffled grunt of effort and the tiny *ching* of metal against metal.

Burglar? The lights were off, the truck was gone, it was Saturday night. Possible.

Vivian crept to the edge of the roof, keeping low. Her eyes narrowed, her claws grew, and her smile was thin and vicious. Burglar Bill would take some stripes home.

She lifted her hand to strike as a head rose over the eaves.

"You!" She snatched her hand back.

"Vivian, you scared the piss outta me."

Aiden pulled himself over the gutter and onto the roof.

Text

COM9098407A
9781442014817
L40664000000

[1]RFID 3M

YA KLAUSE

Blood and chocolate /
R0202881389

R0202881389

7

"Surprise!" Aiden said.

Vivian swallowed a growl. *No shit.*

"What are you doing here?" she managed to choke out as she sat back on her haunches. She trembled with the strain of holding back the change.

"I thought you'd be happy to see me," Aiden said.

"You startled me," she muttered, sorry about the hurt in his eyes.

His velvet smile forgave her. "I thought if you couldn't get to the party, I'd bring the party to you." He crawled to her side and shrugged off his backpack. She almost pulled away but the richness of his smell held her close against her will. "I wasn't expecting to find you on the roof," he said. "I was gonna knock on your window." He unbuckled the backpack and pulled out a bottle of wine.

Dear Moon, he's sweet, Vivian thought in anguish. A swift pang hit her gut, and she bit the inside of her cheek, hoping the pain would keep her sane. *Not sweet like that,* she screamed silently, staring with panicked eyes at his round firm thighs.

After the wine came two glasses wrapped in a bandanna, then a chunk of cheese, a plastic knife, and some paper napkins left over from Christmas.

"Classy, huh?" Aiden's eyes glittered with delight.

She licked her lips nervously. "Lovely. You brought dinner," she heard herself say. She wanted to bolt for the woods. *You fool,* she thought. *You shouldn't have come.*

She glanced at the moon. It was still behind the trees, its light mercifully broken by foliage so that she and Aiden were covered by mottled shadow. Could he see any change in her? Aiden was cutting slices of cheese onto the bandanna, babbling away. He didn't seem to notice anything wrong.

She experienced a dizzying surge of pain and pleasure and her face twitched. Her hands flew to her ears and felt them push past her fingers. She hastily pulled her hair around her face.

How do I make him go? she thought as her joints began to pop.

"Here you go." He held a slice of cheese to her mouth and it was all she could do not to take his fingers off. The cheese was sharp and ripe and clung to her tongue. She sluiced it down with the glass of wine he offered.

"Hey, silly, you're supposed to sip," he said. "I don't want you doing something you'll regret later." His eyes suggested otherwise.

Her lips raised into what she hoped was a smile; then she turned away swiftly. How were her teeth?

64

He moved closer and put an arm around her. "You pick a funny time to go shy on me," he said.

Her shoulders shook with silent laughter at her stupidity. How could she think she could be intimate with a human? She detected an undeniable rippling up her spine, and a hardness came to her eyes and the corners of her mouth. She tested a new idea. *So what if I hurt him?*

"Vivian?" Aiden whispered. His breath was light on her cheek, fragrant with the warm wine and cheese.

It was a stupid thought. She doubled over and moaned. "I'm sorry, I'm so sorry."

"What's wrong?" Aiden asked, surprise and concern in his voice.

"I think I'm coming down with the flu," she said. What a brainstorm. "Maybe you should go. I don't want you to catch it."

"But someone should look after you if you're ill."

"I'd rather be alone," she insisted through clenched teeth.

Still he didn't move to go.

"What's wrong with you, boy?" she cried. "Do you *like* watching people throw up?"

His eyes widened.

She felt like a jerk. She changed her tone. "Please. I'll be embarrassed if you stay."

"But—"

A spasm ripped through her and the bones in her knees crunched. "Go! Please go!" she yelled, and scrambled for the window like a drunk, her legs refusing to obey. "I'm going to be sick."

She dove onto her bed, rolled to the floor, and spidered out of the room on knuckles and toes. She reached the bathroom at the end of the hall and slammed the door behind her. She shot the bolt home.

Outside the window the swollen moon leered at her over the tops of the trees.

She shuddered with pain, and tears outlined her downy face. She had never known a time when she hadn't wanted the change, hadn't enjoyed the change, but now she was nauseated from holding it back. He couldn't see her like this. She couldn't betray her people.

There was a gentle tapping on the bathroom door. "Are you all right?"

She tried to say *Yes, I am,* but her jaw was wrong for speaking and the words came out a muffled growl. Why was he making this beautiful gift seem dirty?

"Well, if you're sure you'll be okay . . ."

"Hhhhhhmmmmmmmmmm!" she moaned, hoping it sounded like an affirmative. Her arms lengthened, her muscles bulged, and she tore at her clothes as her pelt rippled over her flesh. She had never had to hide away before. What a crime to trap her beautiful body. It was all his fault.

"Look, like, give me a call tomorrow and let me know how you are. Hope you feel better."

When she was sure he had gone, Vivian quietly pulled back the bolt with short, furred fingers. She reached for the doorknob.

But what if I'm like Axel? she thought. *What if I smell him as prey when I'm in fur?*

She clenched her hand, withdrew her shaking fist,

and curled into a tight, trembling ball on the bathroom floor. *I won't go out,* she promised. *I won't go out.* If she did, she might follow him and stalk him to his lair.

She shuddered into her final shape, raised her muzzle, and howled frustration at the porcelain tile. Her voice echoed about her like a curse.

Vivian blinked her eyes in the early-morning sun. The sound of a truck door slamming had awakened her. Esmé and Rudy were back. She sneezed, sending dust mice scurrying, and crawled, pink and naked, out from under the bed, where she'd spent most of the night. She was drained and aching from clenching her body tight against its needs.

I'll have to tell him I can't see him anymore, she thought. *I can't hide from him every full moon.* She tried to feel self-righteous and committed, but all she felt was a sinking feeling in her gut. He had climbed up to her window, brought her wine, thought of her when he could have been out partying. She remembered the tickle of his hair on her cheek, his breath on her neck, and shivered deliciously.

Vivian reached for her robe, which lay in a silken gray-and-blue shimmer across her desk chair, and dragged a brush through her tangled tawny hair. *No,* she told herself firmly. *I'll leave the poor boy alone.* How long before the Five bothered him because of her? How long before the pack stepped in? They wouldn't be leaderless forever. Soon there would be someone to answer to. That last thought annoyed her. Maybe she didn't want to answer to someone.

"Perhaps Astrid's right," Esmé said as Vivian walked into the kitchen.

"What do you mean?" asked Rudy from the counter, where he was pouring the coffee.

"Why aren't females allowed to compete in the Ordeal?" Esmé said. She sat at the kitchen table. There was a leaf in her hair, and Vivian was jealous of Esmé's night in the open.

"Gimme a break!" exclaimed Rudy. "Isn't it obvious? It's purely physical. Females are in a different weight category. Their muscles don't develop to the same degree. Why risk injury or death with no chance to win?"

Vivian took the cup of coffee meant for her mother from Rudy's hands and leaned back against the counter to drink it. Rudy rolled his eyes, but poured another cup.

"But some females are smarter than some males, craftier fighters," Esmé argued.

Rudy set Esmé's coffee in front of her and sat down himself. "Stop being awkward, Esmé. It's only a way of matching fairly and protecting our own. You females get your chance. It's only the top female who mates with the victor. She has to be the strongest and the smartest to ensure our survival."

"Yeah, great, some chance. It's a male's world, isn't it? A female may be queen bitch but *she* doesn't get to choose her king."

"You loved Ivan, didn't you, Sis?" Rudy asked. "You didn't beat the crap out of every new girl who came along with a challenge just for the status."

Vivian watched her mother's face closely.

Esmé glanced down, but not before Vivian saw her eyes soften. "Yeah," Esmé said.

"And he loved you. You had his tail between your teeth. Who's to say the queen bitch isn't the real pack leader?"

Yes, Vivian thought. *Mom always got her way with Dad.* But what if she'd wanted the power but not him? She couldn't have had it.

"So you had options," said Rudy. "You didn't have to fight for the leader. A female can choose any other mate as long as he'll have her."

"That's a mockery," Vivian said, startling them. "The match still has to be pack approved, and she isn't even allowed to whelp without the permission of the leader. What kind of choice is that?"

"Well," Rudy said, amusement in his eyes. "I didn't know we had another rebel in the house."

Esmé laughed. "She's a teenager, for Moon's sake. She's supposed to rebel."

Vivian bristled. How easily they dismissed her feelings as a stage she was going through. Her mouth closed into a thin line.

Esmé grinned and winked at Vivian. "Never mind, babe. I'm sure we won't dare deny you when you make your choice. You'd make our lives too miserable."

Yeah? Vivian thought. *I might surprise you.* She glared at her mother and drank in silence. *Dammit, there's no reason I should let pack traditions rule me,* she decided. *The Law is supposed to keep us safe and strong and able to birth healthy children, yet the Law wants us to tear each other apart to find a leader. The Law's a bunch of hypocrisy.*

In her room, relaxed after a shower, Vivian stood in the breeze of her fan, enjoying the coolness of air on her wet skin. She smiled lazily, imagining fingers trailing instead of water drops. *There must be a way to cope with Aiden,* she thought. *There has to be.*

But was Aiden angry with her after last night? She had ruined his surprise. The boys she had known in the past would have been pissed. But then, he wasn't like the boys she had known, was he? That was the point.

She walked down the hall to the phone.

8

"Why does he have to drag parents into this?"
Vivian grumbled as she ransacked her closet.

Aiden's family were having their first cookout of the
season to celebrate the end of school, and Aiden had
invited her along.

"It'll just be casual," he'd told her.

Casual! What was so casual about being inspected
by parents?

The weather was too hot for jeans, so she pulled out
a scarlet tank dress. Parents liked girls in dresses,
didn't they? She wanted them to like her, for his sake.
She wiggled into the sheath of cotton and swept her
thick hair back with combs. But that didn't mean she
couldn't dress for him, too.

Rudy shook his head when he saw her come downstairs. "God help the poor bastard, whoever he is."

Aiden honked outside, and she hurried out before
Esmé could have a chance to see who she was leaving with.

She was pleased with Aiden's low whistle when he

saw her, and not even the kiss she gave him could completely wipe the silly grin off his face.

Vivian could smell the aroma of charcoal as soon as they pulled to the curb in front of a large brick, ivy-covered house. Aiden led her through a white picket side gate and past the kitchen steps to the backyard. On a crazy-paved patio a thin, slightly balding man in a striped apron was poking at the embers under the grill.

"Hi, Dad!" Aiden called.

The man looked up, waved a spatula at his son in greeting, and then saw Vivian. His mouth opened a fraction wider, and he raised his eyebrows. He recovered quickly. "You're Vivian?"

"Pleased to meet you," she answered.

"Well, you're an improvement," Mr. Teague said, and laughed.

"Dad!" Aiden looked mortified.

"He usually goes for the combat boots and black eyeliner types," Aiden's father explained. "I'm glad he's brought home someone normal for a change. His girlfriends usually scare the hell out of me."

"Stop embarrassing your son." An attractive woman, older than Vivian's mother, came down the kitchen steps, carrying a tray. A skinny girl in pink shorts, about thirteen years old, followed her with soda bottles under each arm. The girl eyed Vivian boldly.

"This is my mom," Aiden said, "and my sister, Ashley."

"We're happy you could come," Mrs. Teague said, but her smile was brittle as she took in Vivian head to toe. She put her tray on the picnic table.

"Yeah," said Ashley. "Sure." She dumped the big plastic bottles beside the tray, then flopped into a recliner and dragged the earphones around her neck back to her ears.

"Ashley, there are people present," her father called over.

Ashley closed her eyes in response, and Mrs. Teague sighed in exasperation. "Want a Coke?" she asked Vivian.

"Yes, please. Great."

"How do you like your burger?" asked Mr. Teague.

"Rare, thank you," Vivian answered. She sat on the other recliner and crossed her legs. Aiden sat on the flagstones at her side. She could tell Mr. Teague was sneaking peeks at her. Aiden was too busy looking at her himself to notice.

Aiden's parents were polite enough, but she didn't feel as if she was being welcomed as part of the family or anything; she was more of a curiosity. She felt vaguely worried. Would they change Aiden's mind about her?

The meal was served with small talk at the picnic table. Aiden took every chance he could to touch her, brushing her fingers when he handed her a fork, wiping some crumbs from her face, nudging her with his shoulder when he made a joke. Vivian noticed that his mother looked away when he did this, as if his affection bothered her.

Vivian told the edited version of her background. Mrs. Teague was thrilled at the concept of running a country inn. She had the impression that Esmé must be very chic. "You must introduce me to your mother," she said. *Yeah,* Vivian thought. *I know you'd love to go with her to a biker bar and get into a friendly fistfight over some guy with "Suck My Crankshaft" tattooed over his heart.*

"I expect you're proud of Aiden's poem in *The Trumpet,*" she said to change the subject.

Ashley burst out laughing.

Mr. Teague stabbed another burger from the serving plate. "I would have preferred a team picture in the yearbook." It had the smell of an old argument.

Vivian expected some words of support from Aiden's mother, but none came.

Aiden concentrated on his food, but his cheeks were flushed. Vivian wanted to leave and take him with her.

When they'd finished eating, Aiden helped his mother take the dishes inside. Mrs. Teague looked surprised, and Vivian knew that Aiden must be on his best behavior.

Mr. Teague glanced over at his daughter, lost again in her Walkman, before he addressed Vivian. "Um, so, what's a gorgeous girl like you doing with my son?" he asked.

She was tempted to say *He's great in bed,* just to see Mr. Teague's face, but she didn't. "He's pretty gorgeous himself."

"He'd be better-looking if he'd cut that damn hair. I would think a girl like you would go out with someone older." He winked at Vivian.

Like someone your age? Vivian thought, repelled by the man's lack of loyalty to his son. She gave him a sultry look. "Well, some older men are attractive," she said in a purposely breathy voice, and watched him puff up like a rooster, "but I haven't met any for a while."

Luckily Aiden and Mrs. Teague came back before Mr. Teague figured out whether or not she'd insulted him, and Ashley removed her headphones to ask in a bored tone when dessert was coming.

"I'm gonna show Vivian my room," Aiden said.

Ashley perked up. "Whoa-oh-oh."

"Do you think that's quite proper?" his mother asked.

"Gimme a break," he mumbled. "You're all down here, aren't you?"

"I don't know why you'd want to show that room to anyone," Mr. Teague said. "But don't be long or we'll send the posse after you." He laughed self-consciously.

Aiden relaxed the moment they were alone. He nuzzled and kissed her all the way up the stairs while she squirmed and tried not to giggle too loudly. She wished his family was a thousand miles away.

"I'm sorry I mentioned the poem," she said.

He shrugged. "That's all right."

The woodwork in his room was painted black, and so were the radiators and the ceiling. The walls were covered with posters and hooks from which dangled such things as beads, tassels, and a fake shrunken head made from an apple. "My mom wouldn't let me paint the walls black," Aiden explained. "She said it would be hard enough painting over the ceiling when I finally left home, so I gave her a break."

I'll bet, Vivian thought, imagining the fight they must have had. "I'm painting my room, too." She told him about the mural.

He laughed. "I guess your mom's not too thrilled, either."

She shook her head. "Cute," she said, examining a plastic model of Godzilla that marched across the top of his black dresser, followed by half a dozen smaller Godzillas.

"Momzilla," Aiden said.

Next to the Godzilla family was a mound made of plasticine topped by a crucifix. She suspected it was meant to be a grave. A tiny doll's hand poked through the surface, like a corpse emerging.

"You've got a warped sense of humor, boy," she said.

Aiden laughed with her. "My aunt Sarah gave me the cross. It's real silver. She thinks I'm going to hell."

"Why's that?" Vivian asked. It seemed strange that one of his own pack would damn him like that.

"Oh, my long hair, I listen to Satanic music, and I have an unhealthy curiosity. She suggested to my mother that she burn my books."

"No!"

"Honest."

She walked over to have a look at those dangerous works of literature in his bookcase. Most were horror and fantasy novels, but at the end of the middle row sat *A Witches' Bible Complete* and *The Druid Tradition*. An Aleister Crowley paperback lay open, facedown on the top shelf.

"You believe this stuff?" she asked.

He looked relieved that there was no sarcasm in her voice. "Well, curious really. I mean, we shouldn't close ourselves to possibilities right?"

So he liked to be open to possibilities, huh? Was he open enough to accept the truth about her? There was a thought. Would he still care for her if he knew?

"You read Tarot?" she asked, picking up a pack of cards. It was the classic Rider-Waite deck.

"I haven't learned yet. I've got something about it here, though." He shuffled through some books.

"That's okay," she said. "I only wondered. My great-aunt uses that deck." It was easier to call Persia Devereux that than to explain. A pack was like family, and all older members were aunts and uncles. "She's very good."

"Cool. Your aunt reads Tarot. What other neat stuff does your family do?"

Wouldn't you like to know? she thought.

"That's a wicked smile." He put his arms around her. "Are you getting ideas now I've got you in my den of iniquity?"

Den. She liked his choice of words. "And what ideas would I be getting?"

"Something like this." His lips met hers, and his hand slid up to cup her left breast gently. She put her own hand over his and made him squeeze harder as her tongue snaked into his mouth. Why did he always have to be so damn polite?

He moaned. *That's better,* she thought. *Loosen up, boy.*

"Dessert time!" Ashley's voice echoed up the stairwell.

"Oh, man." Aiden kissed her neck. "Better go, or

she'll come and get us." His voice was husky. Vivian loved hearing him sound that way. "You go on down," he said, releasing her. "I've got to do a couple of things."

Yeah, like pour a glass of cold water down your shorts, she thought, and grinned. "See you soon," she whispered, and slinked out in a way that she knew would keep him up there a few extra minutes.

After dessert, Vivian excused herself. "I need to use the bathroom," she explained.

"Aiden, show Vivian the rest room in the basement, will you, so she doesn't have to go traipsing upstairs again," Mrs. Teague said.

To keep me away from his bedroom, you mean, Vivian thought. When Vivian had come downstairs, Mrs. Teague had stared at her as if Aiden had left handprints all over her dress.

Aiden took Vivian through a door into a workroom. Guns hung on the wall and a workbench was scattered with parts and tools.

"Dad's hobby," Aiden explained. "He collects and repairs antique guns."

Vivian was fascinated. "What's that?" she asked, pointing to some equipment on the bench.

"He makes his own bullets for some of them," Aiden said.

"Isn't that hard?"

Aiden shook his head. "No. He taught me."

Vivian was surprised. "I wouldn't think you were into guns."

"I'm not. That was a long time ago. He used to take me out hunting," Aiden said. "You know, like a 'real American' father and son are supposed to do. I hated it. There should be more to being with your father than going out and killing something together."

Vivian didn't speak. She'd give anything to be able to go out and kill something with her father again. This made her feel sadly distant from Aiden. She took his hand from her waist. "I'll meet you back outside," she said.

"Oh, yeah. The bathroom. Over there." He pointed to a door near the stairs.

Coming out of the bathroom, Vivian heard voices upstairs from the direction of the kitchen.

"She seems rather sophisticated for Aiden, don't you think?" said Mrs. Teague.

"She does seem mature." Vivian could hear the innuendo in Mr. Teague's voice. It made her skin crawl.

"You watch yourself." Mrs. Teague didn't sound amused. "You'd better have a talk with that boy."

Vivian heard the sound of a screen door closing. *Have a talk with him about what?* she wondered. What had she done wrong? Why did Mrs. Teague not want a mate for her son?

The rest of the visit was ruined for Vivian.

"Your parents don't like me," she said on the way home.

"That's a good sign," Aiden said. "They don't like any of the people I care for."

But it wasn't only his parents.

Vivian took a deep breath. "People weren't friendly at school, either," she said. "Is there something wrong with me?"

"God, no!"

Aiden didn't say anything else for a while, but just when she thought he had nothing to add to the topic, he spoke. "You're, like, so beautiful and cool and sure of yourself, I think the kids at school were frightened of you."

"Frightened of me?" Vivian laughed with surprise. These people didn't have enough sense to know what to be frightened of. She could show them frightening.

"Well, you know," Aiden continued. "Afraid that maybe you wouldn't tolerate lesser mortals, so why bother."

They pulled up in front of her house. "So, are you afraid of me?" she asked, trying to keep the amusement from her voice.

"Terrified," he said as he reached for her.

Vivian stopped him with a gentle touch. "Why weren't you like the others? Why didn't you freeze me out when I talked to you the first time?"

He studied her while he thought. "Well, apart from the fact that you're the most beautiful girl I've ever seen, curiosity, I suppose."

"Curiosity?"

He looked down into his lap as if shy of telling her. "Until you drew that pentagram in my palm, then I knew we could be friends. That you might be . . ." He bit his lip and flung his head back, eyes closed. "Oh, man. This sounds dumb."

He was so endearing. She leaned over and touched the tip of her tongue to his cheek. "What does?"

"That you could be my soul mate." He said it fast, looking everywhere but at her. "That I could bare everything to you and you would understand."

Vivian was stunned. He was exposing his belly to her. A rush of warmth filled her. "Sweet puppy," she said. "Bare everything and you would certainly have my undivided attention." Her tongue touched his ear.

"You're making fun," he said, his anxious eyes finally meeting hers.

She sat up straight. "No, I'm not. I'm honored," she answered seriously. She didn't want to hurt his feelings.

He relaxed and the smile came back to his eyes. "See you tomorrow?" he asked.

"Yeah."

Was she Aiden's soul mate? Vivian wondered up in her room. Wouldn't she know if she were? Maybe if she made him the mate of her flesh first, then she would know.

9

They were always at parties, or at the movies, or hanging out at someone's house, always in the midst of Aiden's friends, the Amoeba. Even when they were alone together he was very careful in how far he went, as if he was afraid to scare her off. This made her smile. *Soon, baby, I'll let you know how scared I'm not,* she thought.

Then one evening, when he took her home, Aiden had bad news. "I have to go on vacation with my parents." He flushed with embarrassment as he told her. "I thought I could get out of it," he said. "I'm too old to get dragged to the beach with Mommy and Daddy. But they went on and on, you know, about how I'll be in college soon and it's our last chance to have a family vacation together, blah, blah, blah." He smiled anxiously at her. "I'll miss you."

"And my birthday," Vivian said sulkily, then immediately felt bad because he looked so stricken. She kissed his cheek, letting her lips linger there as she whispered a kind of apology. "Never mind, bring me back a shell or something." She could feel his skin grow hot as he responded to the warm flutter of her breath.

"I'll be back just in time for the Fourth of July," he promised, slipping his arms around her. "We'll go see the fireworks at the park. I bet someone's having a party." Someone was always having a party.

Apparently there wasn't to be a birthday fuss this year. Vivian found presents from Rudy on the kitchen table with a note explaining he would be out late and, after tossing her own contribution down, Esmé went off humming to talk on the phone for hours. *Thanks for sticking around to see if I like it,* Vivian thought as she unwrapped a silky blouse. Once her birthdays had been celebrated by all the pack.

At eight that evening the doorbell rang. "Go answer it," Esmé called from upstairs. "It's my date."

Great, Vivian thought. *She's leaving me alone on my birthday.*

But when she opened the door the Five surged in. They swept her back to the living room with hugs and licks and love bites and cries of "Happy birthday!" Gregory carried a big paper bag stuffed with packages.

Esmé ran down the stairs, giggling. "A woman should have plenty of men around on her birthday," she declared.

The doorbell rang again and Esmé went to answer it this time. She came back with Gabriel.

Oh, I get it, Vivian thought. *Bring your own babe.*

But Esmé looked surprised. She swept her hair back with long fingers and managed to undulate while standing still. "Gabriel." Her voice was suddenly husky. "Come to take me somewhere good." She crooned the last word.

"I came to wish Vivian happy birthday," he said.

"How nice," Esmé said, dropping the purr.

Great Moon, he's politicking, Vivian thought, *like he has to win votes for leadership instead of win a fight.* "Kissing babies?" she asked.

"I'd hardly call you a baby," he replied, looking her over with a grin.

Jerk, she thought.

Esmé ran to the kitchen and came back with a six-pack of Coke and two bags of chips, which she dumped on the coffee table. That was her idea of being a good hostess.

Rafe rolled his eyes when Vivian passed him a Coke. He took a big gulp; then, as soon as he thought Esmé and Gabriel weren't looking, he took a small flask from his back pocket and added an amber fluid to the can.

Gregory tipped the contents of the bag he carried onto the table beside the refreshments. "Presents," he declared unnecessarily, and settled his gangly frame upon the couch. Vivian noticed he was growing sideburns. He'd grow a small beard soon, she knew. He always copied Rafe.

While Esmé exclaimed over the tumbled pile of gifts, Ulf fidgeted and nudged till Rafe handed him the flask. Gabriel saw this time. He didn't say anything, but his lip rose in a snarl. *Who died and made you God?* Vivian thought. Rafe glowered back defiantly, but he put the flask away. Ulf pouted, his red locks falling around his face.

"Aren't you going to open your presents?" Finn asked.

Vivian gave in and picked up a parcel. Inside she found a scant, lacy slip. "Don't tell me," she said. "You went shoplifting at Victoria's Secret." The Five collapsed into hysterics, and Willem pushed another gift into her hands. Esmé and the boys howled with laughter as Vivian opened box after box of provocative gauzy underwear.

"Try them on," Willem urged as she held aloft another pair of frilly panties.

"Yeah, we wanna make sure they fit," said Finn, grabbing them from his twin.

"In your dreams, wolf-boy," said Vivian.

The smirk on Gabriel's face at her words made her seethe. She could put Finn down; he couldn't. What was he doing hanging out here anyway? He'd made his public appearance. Why didn't he leave?

She deliberately tried to make him feel he didn't belong by ignoring him and kissing all the Five thank you, despite their jeers and rude suggestions. Gregory put on some music—the hard pounding kind the Five loved—and she danced with them all except Gabriel. She was surprised to find she was having a good time.

Esmé glowed with contentment. She didn't even

seem to be disappointed when Gabriel would only dance one dance with her. Instead she plied him hopefully with Jack Daniel's on the rocks.

Later, Vivian was rinsing some glasses in the sink when she felt someone behind her. Arms snaked around her. Hands came down over her breasts and squeezed rudely. She recognized the small spider tattoo on the right hand.

"Get off, Rafe," she said, continuing to swish hot water in the tumbler she held.

"Come on. You love it."

"Like hell."

"I don't see you running," he said, and she felt his hot breath on her neck and his teeth testing her flesh.

Vivian put the glass on the counter. She twisted slowly around into his accommodating arms, face to face with his arrogant leer.

His grin widened. "I knew it."

She smiled back at him. Her hand traveled up his thigh and his eyes grew vacant with lust, his lips parted, waiting for hers.

That was when she grabbed his crotch and squeezed.

"Ahwooooooo!" he yanked at her wrist with both hands.

"Ah, come on. You love it," she said, gripping tighter.

"Lemme go!"

Esmé called from the living room. "What's going on?"

Vivian glanced toward the door. She was startled to see Gabriel standing there. His eyes sparkled with laughter and his teeth gleamed white.

Vivian released Rafe. "Nothing, Mom. Just fooling around. Huh, Rafe?"

Rafe didn't say anything. He turned and sucked in a whimper of embarrassed rage when he saw Gabriel. He stalked out of the kitchen, his face clenched in anger.

"You can take care of yourself," Gabriel said, nodding in appreciation.

"And don't you forget it," Vivian answered. She caught the tangy whiff of his sweat as she swept by him, and felt a brief surge of fear mixed in with the heady tingle of sweet defiance. Maybe he would swat her for her insolence. Instead she heard a throaty chuckle.

She shouldn't have encouraged the Five. All the next week they were at the door or on the phone. She wouldn't run with them at night, but she finally gave up and spent some daylight time with them. Mostly they hung out and traded jokes with the bikers in front of Tooley's bar. Once they went to the mall, and the five cracked each other up menacing middle-school girls by wiggling long, long tongues at them. Vivian left in disgust.

The Five's continual bickering and jostling for rank got on her nerves. It was a relief to pick up the phone one day and hear Aiden's voice.

"Ready for fireworks?" he asked.

"Baby, are you?" she replied.

It was still light when Aiden arrived the next evening. He looked sleek and suntanned. Vivian wanted to bite the buttons off his shirt.

"I missed you," he said, and handed her a small, brightly wrapped package.

Vivian turned it over and over in her hands, admiring it as if it were a jewel. Was this the shell she had asked for? No one outside the pack had ever bought her a present. How exquisite and full of promise it was.

"You're supposed to open it," Aiden prompted gently.

"Oh, yeah." Vivian sliced through the tape with her nails and peeled off the paper, slowly savoring each crackle. Inside was a velvet box. "Ooooh!" She stroked its plushness, delayed a second more, then opened the box and found a sparkling silver pentagram on a silver chain.

Vivian was speechless for a moment; then she burst into laughter. He had given her silver.

When paired with wolf-kind blood, silver burned through the flesh like acid, doing more damage than even her people's amazing powers of healing could stop. That was why silver bullets were often fatal no matter where or how slight the wound. Silver was safe enough to wear as long as it didn't touch an open wound, but among her kind fights were common. Wolf-kind preferred to wear gold, just in case.

A legend told of the double-edged gift of Lady Moon, who gave them the ability to change, but also turned her light into the silver that could kill them if they abused the power. Aiden had given her a double-edged gift: the sign of her people made out of poison.

Aiden looked mystified by her laughter, then hurt. "You don't like it," he said.

I could wear it on our dates, at least, she decided. That seemed safe enough. "Yes, I do like it," she said solemnly. "It's more perfect than I could ever tell you."

Because I, too, have a double edge, she thought. *And you should run from me as fast as your legs can carry you.*

JULY

Thunder Moon

10

They left Aiden's car outside her house; it would be hard to find a parking spot close to the middle-school field where the fireworks display was held. The Fourth of July festival had been going on all day, starting with the parade and continuing with clowns, competitions, races, and music. The best places to park had been claimed hours before.

"Let's go the back way," Vivian said. "It's quicker."

They cut through her yard and followed the river upstream. The sun was going down and the evening was golden. Vivian inhaled deeply, as if she could suck it all in and keep it forever. The rich bursts of odor released by a day of heat mixed with the salty exquisite smell of Aiden swelled her with happiness. As they crashed through the tufted grass to the border mowed alongside the river, Vivian felt the urge to run. "Come on," she cried, and took off full of the joy of breath, her limbs as strong as if she danced on the moon.

When she hurdled a wall to an alley behind some apartments he was a minute behind. She waited until he caught up. He vaulted over, using both arms, and she was sad he'd not leaped as she had, touching nothing but wind. Perhaps he couldn't. Immediately she wanted to give him flight wrapped up in a pretty box like his gift to her. Instead, she gave him a quick hard hug, which made him grunt, then laugh.

The alley led to a bridge. Vivian bounced across beside Aiden, eager to run again. His breathing was coarse, but he didn't complain. A drop of sweat hung at the tip of his nose. She darted her tongue and slurped it off.

"Yugh!" Aiden wiped his nose with the back of his hand, then grinned.

"You don't get enough exercise," Vivian said. "You should run more often."

Aiden rolled his eyes. "Yeah, right."

"No, come on. I'll teach you." She set off again at a steady, slower pace. He groaned behind her, but she heard him follow. As soon as they were in the baseball field she danced around him, giving him advice about breathing and stride. She jogged sedately for a while, enjoying the feel of him running at her side. His face was flushed, and he puffed a bit, but he would learn.

A sparkle crackled between the trees ahead and for a moment she thought the fireworks had started too soon, but it was only the setting sun caught in the school windows, broken up by leaves shimmied in a sudden evening breeze. She glanced behind. The western sky blazed vermilion as if it were drenched in the blood of night, and she choked back a howl of joy.

She had to run loose. She took off, driven by excitement into the arms of the dark.

The grass whipped her ankles; the dusk licked her face. If she ran fast enough she could climb invisible stairs right into the stars. She reached the twelve-foot chain-link fence at the back of the school and threw herself up. She swarmed over with barely a thought.

When Aiden caught up he rattled like chaos climbing the fence, and panted and scrambled and slid.

"When did you go to boot camp?" he managed to gasp when he dropped at her feet. He looked put out but not angry. "Jeez. I didn't know my sweetheart was the Amazon Queen."

Sweetheart. He'd called her his sweetheart. She'd been a main squeeze, an ol' lady, and a piece of tail, but she'd never been a sweetheart before. The word bubbled through her like champagne. She threw herself to the ground, giggling. "I'm exhausted," she lied.

He tried to gently wrestle her to her feet but she kept on sliding limply from his arms, and soon they were a giggling puppy tumble in the grass. His sweet wet kisses made her sure he wasn't angry, and he was out of breath again, but for reasons he couldn't complain about.

They walked into the gathering crowd tangled in each other's arms and hair, their lips unable to stay apart.

The Amoeba was down by the edge of the tarmac playground, spilling into the forbidden field where the fireworks were set up. Some of them called greetings when they saw Aiden and Vivian arrive. Kelly smiled tightly, her eyes shallow. She leaned back to her regular troupe of gigglers and said something for their ears alone. Vivian clicked her teeth in Kelly's direction, wrinkling her nose, and grinned wickedly when Aiden pulled her down with him to a tartan blanket and nuzzled her neck. *Look at me, Kelly,* Vivian gloated silently. *I've got him. You don't. Too bad.*

One of the guys handed Aiden a Coke. Aiden sipped, grimaced, and handed it to Vivian. "All yours if you want. I've got to drive later." Vivian took a swig. The Coke was laced with rum and sent a delicious fire rippling to her toes. She drank some more and held the bottle tight.

Every so often a tired-looking cop would walk by and tell them to get their butts back onto the yard, and the Amoeba would mutter and move blankets around and make a great show of activity and eventually not move an inch.

"Yo, buddy!" Aiden's best friend, Peter Quincey, arrived, pounding Aiden's back and calling greetings to everybody. Two of the gigglers peeled away from Kelly and fawned on him. Girls always wanted to touch him and hug him.

Then Bingo and Jem showed up, arguing loudly about which bands sucked. They soon got everyone involved.

"Hey, I've got to take a leak," said Aiden. "I better go now, before the fireworks start." He stood up after kissing her cheek.

"So what do you think of The Purge?" Jem asked her.

"Bunch of whiners," she answered. "They should be drowned to put them out of their misery."

One of the gigglers shrieked indignantly and Quince roared with laughter. This started a whole new round of the argument. The rum made Vivian feel lazy and indulgent. She actually agreed with Kelly once.

A firefly bumbled past Vivian on a mission of love and the brightness of its tail announced that night had arrived. As if everyone realized this at once, the crowd hushed in expectation. Men scurried around the field, making last-minute checks.

Aiden had been gone a long time.

In the sudden quiet, a chorus of howls echoed like a distant song in the trees beyond the portable toilets.

Bingo smirked. "Someone's having fun."

"Yeah," Vivian agreed, and the fine hair on her spine prickled. She stared grimly over the heads of the crowd. Aiden was out there alone. The blood in her veins turned cold. "I think I need to pee, too," she announced to no one in particular. She set her bottle down and hurried off in the same direction Aiden had gone.

She wove through the islands of families and friends stretched out with their coolers and hampers and kids, and tried not to step on the fingers and drinks that spread into the paths that led through the mess. Then she was out the other side.

She could smell the toilets before she even came close. They'd been used all day, and now the rank stench of chemicals mixed with urine and feces made a battlefield of the air. Her nose pinched in distaste as she skirted the metal booths stenciled with the word *Port-o-let* in luminous orange, looking for signs of Aiden, or of the Five.

Someone's cough echoed inside one of the putrid sarcophagi, but it was too deep to be Aiden's. The door of a toilet opened, then crashed shut behind a stranger. The rest of the toilets didn't seem occupied.

She heard faint movement in the woods. What if he'd decided that the toilets stank too badly and had gone to piss in the woods? She'd have thought it sensible any other night, but tonight, with the Five on the prowl . . .

Vivian slunk silently into the trees, her eyes wide and luminous. *He'd better be safe,* she thought. Without even thinking, she lengthened her nails, and the muscles of her limbs clenched with power.

The moon was only a sliver in the western sky. The woods were deep with shadows. Somewhere behind her was an eager crowd, waiting for the night to bloom with fire, but somehow their voices were muffled by the dark. Even the crickets held their breaths.

A staccato crackle came from the river—firecrackers. A dog barked far away. Sweat trickled from Vivian's armpits down past her breasts. She trod on tiptoes, her feet remembering paws.

There was a rustling off to her right. Someone was pushing between the rhododendron bushes. He hummed cheerfully. She almost breathed a sigh of relief, but then she recognized the voice.

"Rafe."

He froze in the shadows. Something almost as big

98

as he was was flung over his shoulder. He clutched it possessively.

Vivian placed the tune he'd been humming. It was an Oingo Boingo song. The words went *walking with a dead man over my shoulder.*

"What have you got there?" she demanded, fear fluttering in her belly.

Rafe's arms tightened around his load. "Nothing." He backed away a step.

"You shithead." She advanced on him. Her heart thumped with dread.

"It's mine," he growled. He slid his kill from his shoulder and let it crash into old, dead leaves. He crouched, ready for combat, in front of it.

Great Moon, I'm right, she thought. *It's a body.* Not Aiden, she begged. She'd kill Rafe if it was.

"I'll share if you're nice to me," he added, a new note of cunning in his voice.

"Show me," she coaxed. "I want to see if it's worth my time."

"Ha, you're lying, Viv," he spat. His eyes glittered and narrowed with malice. "Want to see if it's your meat-boy, Viv?"

The asshole was toying with her. She took another quick step forward but he blocked her, laughing.

She darted to the right, but Rafe was in front of her again.

"Does Vivi want her plaything?" he taunted, and she wanted to shove his pointy teeth down his throat.

She feinted to the left; then, before he could recover, hit him head-on and knocked him down. Distantly the crowd cheered with the first thunder of fireworks. She scrambled over Rafe as he thrashed, elbowing his neck, kneeing him in the stomach, and crawled into the bushes.

In an orange burst of light she saw brown eyes already glazed over with an opalescent sheen. Brown eyes in a furred face. A large dog with its throat torn open lay on the ground.

Rafe scrambled to his feet, laughing. "Had you going, didn't I?"

His laughter was echoed from the trees, and the rest of the Five slunk into the clearing—Finn, Willem, Gregory, and skittery Ulf. Their faces flickered with multicolored light for a moment, etching them with ghoulish shadows. Had they all been out there watching, laughing at her?

The gaping throat leered up at her, black and clotted.

"Smell yummy, Viv?" Rafe mocked. "Think you might like a little taste, since it's not your boyfriend?"

She spat a curse at him as she stood up. It was punctuated by another crash in the sky. She walked right up and knocked him flying with a cuff to the side of the face that left claw marks.

Willem gasped, and Ulf ran back to the bushes giggling hysterically.

Finn helped Rafe up while Gregory glanced back and forth between Vivian and Rafe, nervously licking his lips.

Rafe wiped the blood from his face with the back of

his hand. "You think you're different from us," he snarled. "But you're not. We know who *we* are, Vivian. And we know what we want. We don't run away from it. You're sick, Vivian, if you think you can play human."

He snapped his fingers. "Ulf, get your ass back here and help Greg carry this." The Five fell in silently behind Rafe and followed him into the woods. Only Willem looked back.

"I'm *so* impressed," she yelled after them.

I know who I am, she thought. *How dare he say I don't? I love being* loup-garou. *I adore the sweet change and the beauty it brings me in the night. When I hunt, I hunt wild prey by the laws of the Goddess. I don't kill pets for the fun of it.*

A machine-gun rattle above made her look up to see shooting stars between the leaves. A warbling whistle came fast on its heels and a fountain of fire dripped red in the sky. *I'm missing it,* she thought.

She raced back to the Amoeba, winding through the color-bathed crowd. She found Aiden waiting, and her heart leaped at the sight of him.

"Where did you get to?" Aiden asked. He hugged her.

"I could say the same." She didn't hug back. Now he was safe she could be angry with him—for a moment anyway, until he struggled to make amends with kisses. Then, wrapped in his arms, she oohed and aahed with the faceless multitude around her, made one with them under the bursts of chrysanthemum light.

But danger lurked for the crowd out in the wood,

and she prayed to the Moon that all who watched with her came home safe this night. The Five killed a human once. Did they still have the taste?

The thunder crescendoed. The night was full of whistles and the whoosh of man-made comets. Smoke singed the air and was sharp in her throat, and when she saw sparks falling, she remembered another night more than a year before. *The fire was my fault, too,* she thought. I should have told my father that Axel and the Five were running wild.

She buried her face in her human boy's shoulder and clung to him to suffocate her pain. He kissed her hair, and the tremor of his laughter vibrated through her chest. He was full of rushing blood and smiles and dreams—things her father would never have again.

"I'm sorry," she whispered, too soft for him to hear, but those she spoke to were all dead.

11

On their way back to Vivian's house Aiden stopped by the river. "Don't go home yet," he asked, so they made a nest in the knee-high grass and gazed at the sky.

"Isn't midnight magical?" Vivian asked, and stretched her arms to the stars.

"Not real magic," Aiden said. "I wish it was. Life is a drag most of the time—birth, school, work, death— you know. I wish something magic would happen."

You want magic? I could give you magic, she thought. "What kind of magic?" she asked. "Like finding a door to a magical country? Or a coin that grants wishes? Or meeting a witch?"

Aiden laughed. "All of the above."

"What if she's a wicked witch?"

"Maybe I'd find the good in her."

"What about vampires?"

"I dunno. Maybe there's some good ones, too."

"What about horny werewolves?" Vivian said.

Aiden slid his arms around her. "Now you're being silly."

They sank into the long fur of the river meadow, entwined with each other. The smell of sweet crushed hay filled the air.

"You're wild," Aiden mumbled woozily into the cleft between her breasts before he kissed the mole there.

"Um-hmmm." Vivian stroked his hair, reveling in the way she'd made him drunk with wanting her.

He kissed her mouth, and she returned his kiss fiercely, pressing hard against him, holding him tight by his shirt. Her fingers found a circle behind his pocket—the rolled rim of a rubber encased in foil. A thrill ran through her so sharp and delicious that for a moment she thought she was changing.

With trembling fingers she unbuttoned Aiden's shirt. She smoothed her hands up his firm abdomen and across his chest. His flesh was burning hot and oh so sleek and alien to her touch. She tested his neck with her teeth and tried not to bite too hard. His breath became ragged.

A chorus of howls echoed down the river. A cherry bomb burst in the distance.

Or was it a gun?

Vivian froze.

"Ow! Your nails." Aiden pulled back.

She quickly sheathed her claws. "I'm sorry. I . . ."

Aiden laughed wickedly and reached for her again. "You wild woman."

Vivian felt a vibration in the ground. She struggled to her knees while Aiden held on and murmured in protest. Out in the night a dark mass swept though the grass, coming their way.

"What's wrong?" Aiden asked and rose to kneel beside her.

"It's nothing," she said, and flung her arms around him and carried him to the ground. *That can't be the pack,* she thought. *They wouldn't run in town.* But there were too many to be only the Five.

Aiden rolled over on top of her, and she tried to fake interest. She had to keep him occupied. If he saw what hunted tonight, he might panic and run; if he ran he was prey.

The grass hissed louder and louder as if a storm approached. Voiceless they came—many paws softly thundering.

They passed to the right.

"What the . . ." Aiden sat up.

Vivian snaked an arm around his neck and dragged him back. "Stay down," she told him. "Dogs. They're crazy in packs."

Aiden looked startled. "Jeez, there's a lot."

The musk of them filled the air—familiar scents. Astrid was in the lead. *Damn the bitch.* What was she thinking to lead a run this large through the middle of Riverview?

After Astrid came Lucien Dafoe, Rafe's father, stinking of drink. Rafe was rapidly edging him out. The rest of the Five were there, but so were others, mostly Astrid's age-mates, no elders, and all male. Ulf brought up the rear. She could hear him pant with an asthmatic wheeze.

Then they were past, racing upstream, devouring the night.

105

"Wow," Aiden said. "For a moment I thought it was the wild hunt—Herne the Hunter chasing down the damned."

She could feel the goose bumps on his arm.

"People shouldn't let their dogs run loose like that. Maybe we should call the pound."

"At this time of night?" Vivian said.

He grimaced humorously. "Guess not."

A shout came from up the river.

"Scared someone." Aiden laughed.

Unlike Aiden, she could hear that someone scramble down the bank. Her heart leaped to her throat, but the pack didn't turn to follow the human.

"We should get out of here," she said. "They might come back." And who knew what they'd do if they got the urge for blood on the muzzle? She had to send Aiden home.

Aiden chuckled. "It's not like you to be nervous."

"What do you know about what I'm like?" she snapped. She was sorry instantly, yet irritated by how chastened he looked. Couldn't he fight back? "I'm sorry," she said. "But I don't think it's safe."

He tried to pull her down with him again, unwilling to give up, but the spell was broken, leaving her frustrated and angry. "I have to get home," she lied, removing his hands and standing up. "My mother will worry."

"Oh, man," Aiden said. He climbed awkwardly to his feet, adjusting his clothes. "All right," he grumbled, and she saw him touch his pocket briefly as if bidding his plans goodbye.

Damn. Damn. Damn, she thought.

"What do you mean, tell Gabriel?" Vivian demanded.

It was two in the morning and Rudy had just come home. Esmé was still out the Moon knew where.

"Why him? He hasn't won the Ordeal yet." She had decided not to keep quiet if she saw things going wrong again, but she hadn't expected to tell Gabriel.

Rudy paced the living room. His sturdy compact form and firm stride should have been comforting. "And what did you expect *me* to do?"

"Talk to Astrid. Make her stop."

Rudy laughed bitterly. "That'll be the day."

"So why would she listen to Gabriel, then?" Vivian asked.

"Because she respects him."

"Because she wants to screw him, you mean."

Rudy stared her down with piercing gray eyes that made her feel ashamed. "She respects him because she's afraid of him. Power's the only thing Astrid understands. She isn't sure how far he'll go." He paused. "And neither am I."

"Then why tell him?"

"As far as I can see, he's the only option we've got right now. We can't use a leader who wants to rule with his brains but not his teeth."

Vivian rose to her feet. "My father led with his brains; you mean he wasn't a good leader?"

Rudy ran a callused hand through his hair. His eyes looked sad. "Your father was the best leader we could have had for the time we had him, but this is a time of unrest. We need a leader who understands the power of his jaws."

"I'm tired of violence."

Rudy nodded. "But it doesn't matter what we're tired of, we've got it all the same. You would have never moved the Five so quietly out of West Virginia if Gabriel hadn't beat the sass out of them."

Yeah, thought Vivian. He'd taken them on in the charred ruins of the inn yard when they were set on waging a stupid, hopeless war against the town. Rafe was knocked silly and the others bloodied, but not a scratch on Gabriel. He'd threatened to kill any one of them that moved three paces from the convoy going to Maryland. Smeared with ashes, he'd strutted afterward and she'd hated him for it, even though she'd have beaten the Five herself if she could have. Her father was barely dead, and Gabriel was taking control. He wasn't a leader; her father was a leader. Her father had dignity.

"And when you all arrived," Rudy continued, "Gabriel was one of the first to get a job and put all his money toward getting others settled while he crashed on people's floors or in the woods."

And boy did he smell like it, she thought. *Nothing like a welder with no place to bathe.* "So you're gonna support Gabriel at the Ordeal and not go for it yourself," she said.

"Yeah, guess so. Now, time for bed, babe. Too late to do anything tonight."

Gabriel's black-and-silver motorcycle was in the parking lot of Tooley's bar the next night, exactly as Rudy had guessed. Rudy went in to find him while Vivian waited outside, her arms folded, her foot tapping.

A pair of bikers in cut-off denim jackets over bare chests came out of the bar. The tall one did a double take on her. He grabbed his crotch and issued her a very specific invitation. The other one laughed as if that was the funniest joke he'd ever heard, and his gut jiggled.

She gave them the finger.

"Hey, you're not too friendly," the tall biker complained, changing direction to walk slowly toward her. The smile had left his face. "Ain't you got no respect?"

His buddy trailed him. His grin was mean.

Oh, shit, Vivian thought.

"But tell you what, maybe we could kiss and make up," said the tall biker.

"I'd rather kiss a slug," she said, her temper flaring. She regretted her words when she saw his hands ball into fists. His skull ring glittered ominously.

She felt her legs knot with the first stage of the change. *Control it,* she coached herself. *Only enough to put some muscle on.* She didn't doubt for a moment that she could take them if she changed fully, but she couldn't do that now, could she? A couple of good strong smacks would change his mind.

"I see you've met my sister." Vivian recognized Gabriel's throaty growl.

The tall biker froze for a second, a look of panic on

his face; then he turned. "Hey, Gabe! Your sister, man. Wow. Real pretty girl. I wuz just tellin' her. Yeah. Your sister. Wow."

"Uh, come on, Skull. We got a party to get to," his friend chimed in.

When they turned the corner Gabriel and Rudy burst out laughing.

"I could handle it," Vivian said, annoyed at his amusement.

"I know, baby," he answered, surprising her. "And any other time I would have gladly stood and watched, but Rudy tells me you've got news for me."

"I'll smack him around another time, then," she said.

They walked farther out into the shadowed parking lot. "So, what's the word—little sister?" he asked. She wanted to cut him down for keeping up that sister crap, but the smoldering look in his eyes made her bite back her sarcastic response.

"Astrid led a run along the river last night," she said.

"She did, did she?" His tone was casual but she saw a slight tic in his cheek. "And who was on this run?"

While she listed them he listened with head bowed, stroking the small scar on his lip.

There was silence when she'd finished. She glanced at Rudy, but he was watching Gabriel, a worried look on his face.

Finally Gabriel spoke. "I guess I'll be paying Miss Astrid a little visit," he said softly. He looked up and his pupils caught the glare from a distant streetlight— they glowed red.

What have I started? Vivian thought.

12

Vivian dumped her shopping bag of new paints at the base of the stairs. It fell over, and an economy-sized tube of burnt umber, fat as a sausage, rolled out and rocked gently on the hardwood floor at the edge of the hall rug. The house was so quiet that the muted rumble of the tube's brief passage echoed in her ears. *Where's Esmé?* Vivian wondered. Monday was her day off, but no music blared through the house, and no smell of dinner wafted through the air.

Vivian's answer came when she walked into the living room and was startled to find her mother sitting on the floor surrounded by photographs, more tumbling out of an upturned shoe box beside her.

Esmé looked up with tears in her eyes. "I couldn't remember his face," she said.

Vivian sank to the floor beside Esmé, her mouth tense with worry. There were pictures of her father spread all over the rug: Dad laughing, Dad chopping wood, Dad in the kitchen at the inn, making sauce.

"I tried so hard to forget him so losing him wouldn't

111

hurt anymore," Esmé said, "and then today I thought of him and couldn't see him. It was like I'd torn away a part of me and crippled myself. Like I'd looked into a mirror and couldn't see my reflection." The tears rolled down her cheeks.

Vivian ached to see her mother this upset. She didn't know what was worse, the hard glittering jewel her mother had become this year, or the heartbroken woman beside her now. She couldn't think of anything to say. Instead she picked up a picture of herself at age three, in OshKosh overalls and nothing else, at her father's side as he weeded in the herb garden. She'd been "helping" him, and she could still hear in her mind his patient voice saying, "No honey, not that one." He'd had to say it over and over.

"Dad would have straightened everything out, wouldn't he?" Vivian said. "We wouldn't be in such a mess if he was around."

Esmé shook her head. "I don't know."

Shock cut through Vivian like a sharp little knife. "Sure he would. He'd know how to keep Astrid in line. He'd stop anything bad happening."

"But he didn't, did he?" Esmé said. "The inn burned. People died. If he'd lived, he'd be challenged as unfit."

"That's not true!" Vivian cried.

"You know it's true," Esmé said. "In his wolf-skin he was as strong as any of them, but he was a gentle person in many ways. He'd feel so bad about failing he'd probably step aside for someone else without a fight."

Esmé was right, but for a moment Vivian hated her mother for saying it.

Esmé didn't see Vivian's anger; she was absently shuffling the photos around on the rug as if she could read the future in them like Tarot cards. "Maybe Rudy's right. We need a different kind of leader now. One who doesn't hesitate to hurt if he has to, for the good of all." She reached out a trembling finger and touched the lips of a face that would be nowhere now, ever, except on a square of Kodak paper. "But for his time," she whispered, "oh, he was the best."

Esmé's shoulders heaved in helpless sobs and Vivian's anger shriveled. She put her arms around her mother, buried her face in Esmé's hair, and cried with her in dissonant duet. Esmé clung to her.

There was nothing they could do. He was gone and the world was an alien landscape.

"Let's go out," Esmé said abruptly, wiping the back of her hand across her eyes. "Let's cheer ourselves up." She grabbed Vivian by the shoulders, then planted a quick kiss on her daughter's nose. "We'll treat ourselves to dinner. We deserve it." She leaped to her feet.

Vivian, momentarily confused by her mother's change of mood, didn't answer.

"We'll go to Tooley's and see if any of the pack are there," Esmé said. "But I can only afford burgers."

"I can't do that," Vivian said. "I'm underage."

"Nonsense," Esmé insisted. "As long as you don't drink, no one's gonna throw you out. Especially since you will definitely improve the décor." Esmé smiled proudly at her daughter. "You look just like me."

Vivian couldn't help chuckling. Esmé was her usual arrogant self again. Maybe it would be fun at that.

Maybe she'd enjoy some roughhousing and teasing in the local bar. Maybe she'd like the feel of her palm across the cheeks of some fresh young fool who'd only laugh if off. "Sure, Mom. Let's kick ass."

"It's a deal," Esmé said. "Now I gotta go wash my face. I know I look like shit."

At the door, she paused and turned back to Vivian. There was a slight tremble back in her lower lip. "Thanks, my precious," she said.

There was a scattering of people among the tables and booths at Tooley's; some bikers were at the bar, and four men gathered around the large-screen television watching the Orioles lose. No pack, Vivian thought until they were greeted by an enthusiastic howl from a shadowed corner booth.

"Watch it, Bucky," Esmé warned, hand on hip, but Vivian knew she would have been disappointed if he hadn't noticed.

"You ain't workin' tonight," growled the owner, Terry O'Toole, from behind the bar. "What you doin' here?"

"Can't tear myself away from you, honey," Esmé said, and slid oh so sweet and slinky into a chair.

Vivian saw Tooley color slightly, and saw the twitch of satisfaction on his lips. "She ain't drinkin'," he snapped, pointing at Vivian with a dish towel.

Vivian shrugged. "Not me." She sat down with her mother and crossed her legs in a way she knew made them look a mile long.

"I *know* you're under twenty-one," Tooley added, as if someone had argued with him, and he began to polish the water stains vigorously off a glass no one would look at too closely anyway.

"Hi, Brenda," Esmé said to the waitress who appeared. "We'd like two orders of grease on a bun with all the trimmings. A draft for me and a Shirley Temple for my baby."

"Make that a Coke," Vivian said.

Brenda winked. "Want me to goose that?"

Vivian shook her head. "Nah. The old lady needs to keep her job."

"Old lady!" Esmé squealed, and Brenda left giggling.

It wasn't until they were wiping the crumbs from their mouths that more members of the pack came drifting in, some still yawning from after-work naps, others ready to raise the devil. Tooley's was the place to go, the place to find out where the party was.

Most of the wolf-kind came to Vivian and Esmé's table and greeted them. There was no new leader yet, and Esmé was the widowed queen. *And a tasty morsel, too,* Vivian thought. She could see it in the eyes of the males and the tight smiles of their mates. A female on the loose was a dangerous creature; she could challenge another bitch for a male she fancied. Some of those male eyes strayed to Vivian, too, and she preened at the thought of being a threat. She and Esmé exchanged knowing looks, their lips plump, curved, and smug.

The group around the TV was larger now, swelled

by wolf-kind. Two were males who'd run with Astrid. A cheer went up. The game had turned.

Vivian noted a couple of bikers sauntering over to their table. It was the same two from the other night — Skull and his sidekick. *They never learn,* she thought.

Before the bikers reached the table Bucky was there with two of his buddies — Esmé's age-mates still in their prime. They loomed, they tightened their fists to make their biceps bulge, and they grinned a toothy invitation. The bikers swerved and headed for the exit instead. It was no secret which males usually won any barroom brawl at Tooley's.

As the bikers reached the door it slammed open and they parted hastily to either side.

Lucien Dafoe came stumbling through. He was a mess. Blood covered half his face and still dripped from a gash on his forehead. He clutched his left arm, which dangled uselessly from his side. His shirt front was in tatters, and whatever had shredded it had also shredded his chest. Cotton stuck in the wounds like papier-mâché.

Esmé rose and Vivian with her, her claws unsheathing, heart pounding. Whoever attacked them, she'd be ready. Around the room the pack stood.

"What the fuck happened to you, man?" Skull asked. The other biker gawked through the door. He flinched when a howling devil stormed in — Astrid.

"You coward!" she shrieked at Lucien. "You piece of shit!"

The bikers looked at each other, shock giving way to sniggers.

"What's going on here?" Tooley stepped in front of the bar, a scarred old baseball bat in his hands. A couple of regulars moved to back him. "I don't want you bringing trouble into my place," Tooley said.

"Chill, man," said Bucky. "Family business." He pointed a finger at the bikers and they left in a hurry.

"I'll get you for laughing," Lucien called after them. It was more whine than threat.

The pack drew in from around the room and circled Astrid and Lucien.

"Come on," said Esmé, gripping Vivian's arm tight with excitement, and they joined the others.

Two human women slipped hurriedly out the door. A man trailed after them, casting curious glances back. Some of the others around the bar looked like they would be happy to follow.

"Who did this?" Esmé asked for all of them.

"Who do you think, you asshole?" Astrid spat, and Vivian wanted to smack her.

"Gabriel," Lucien said, almost blubbering. "That bastard, Gabriel."

A hum swept around the circle.

Am I responsible for the state he's in? Vivian wondered. She felt slightly sick.

"Why would Gabriel do that?" Bucky demanded.

" 'Cus he's power mad," Astrid said. "He wants to beat us into following him. Do you want a leader who'd treat us that way?"

Vivian would have agreed with her any other time, but it was Astrid who had risked exposing the whole pack. That was worse than being a bully. She couldn't lead a run that size in the suburbs and expect no one to notice, and if humans noticed . . . Vivian looked around at the humans anxiously. This was too public.

Esmé echoed her thoughts. "This isn't the place, Astrid."

"Who cares what you think, bitch?" Astrid answered.

"I do," said Bucky. His eyes were narrow and dangerous, his clean-shaven face now slightly shadowed. More than half the circle muttered agreement.

Lucien grabbed his side, moaned, and collapsed to the floor. He sat there looking vaguely surprised, a bubble of blood at the corner of his mouth.

"Ain't one of you gonna get him to a hospital?" Tooley called over.

"Yeah, come on," Vivian agreed. They should get out of there before someone phoned the police. They wouldn't be going to the hospital, though; they would take him to Aunt Persia.

One of Bucky's friends put his hands under Lucien's armpits and hauled him up. Bucky grabbed Lucien's legs. They carried him to the door.

The door where Gabriel stood.

Bucky stopped dead. "Hey, man," he said quietly.

Gabriel only nodded. He stood there a moment longer, silent and dark against the glare of a streetlight outside. His fathomless eyes took in the people around the room, daring anyone to challenge him.

"It's not healthy to party with Astrid right now," he finally said in his subterranean growl. "I'd advise against it."

Vivian checked out the others who'd run with Astrid. Their faces were pale and grim. She almost felt sorry for them.

What now? she thought, but when she looked back at the door, Gabriel was gone.

13

"Where are you going, looking so pretty?" Esmé asked.

"I'm meeting Aiden," Vivian told her.

The smile left Esmé's face. "Baby, I know you're lonely for kids your own age, but I wish you'd be careful. If you gotta wag your tail, wag it for one of the Five."

"The Five are jerks."

"But they're *our* jerks. You know what to expect from them."

"I know what to expect from Aiden." She thought of his gentle caresses and his dreams of magic.

"But he'll never know *you*, not really."

Vivian opened her mouth to speak, then clamped it shut.

Esmé must have read the argument in her eyes. "Don't even *think* about telling him about yourself," she said. "That would be the stupidest thing you ever did in your life. If the pack found out, you'd be cast out in case you brought danger back to the den.

How would you like to lose everyone you care about and be alone in the world? And if what you did led to death . . ."

Vivian started toward the door. "I don't want a lecture."

"Honey, I'm just worried," Esmé said. "I get the creeps each time I see that silver around your neck."

Vivian's fingers flew to the pentagram. She had worn it for every date since Aiden had given it to her.

"Listen," Esmé said. "We'll be moving soon. Life will get normal again." She followed Vivian to the door. "You'll have your choice of men. You're beautiful. Don't throw yourself away on someone who can't appreciate you."

"What makes you think he can't appreciate me?" Vivian left the house and slammed the door.

It was one of those steaming days when air clogged the throat like wet cotton wool. *Bloody Moon,* Vivian thought. She wished she hadn't insisted that Aiden not pick her up, but she wanted to keep him away from her house. The smell of the dusty hot sidewalk burned her nose; the sun scorched the top of her head.

Up by Dobb's Corner Store she ran into Rafe with two six-packs of beer in his arms. He wore a clean Nine Inch Nails T-shirt and part of his hair was pulled up in a topknot so he looked like some pagan chief.

"Going to a formal event, then?" Vivian asked him.

"Got me a honey," Rafe said.

She rolled her eyes. "And who's she when she's conscious?"

"You'll see," he said, and sauntered off chuckling.

It wasn't worth puzzling over. She walked on, pleased he was distracted from his insistent pursuit of her.

By the time she reached Aiden's her T-shirt clung to her back and the hair at the nape of her neck was wet. She pushed her leopard-splotched sunglasses back up the bridge of her nose for the millionth time. As she walked up the front path Aiden came rushing out. Before the door closed she heard his father yelling.

"Don't think you can run away from it, my lad."

Aiden grabbed her arm. "Come on," he urged, and tugged her toward his car.

Excited by his firm grip, Vivian yanked the door open and swung herself in. Aiden ran around and climbed into the driver's seat.

The front door opened again. Aiden's father filled the entrance, his face almost purple. "Get back here, young man."

Aiden ground the gears, and they peeled out despite the clanking protests of the old car.

Aiden hit the dashboard with a fist. "Damn!"

Vivian jumped. She'd never seen him this way. She gritted her teeth against the jouncing ride and clung to the sides of her seat. She was sure the car would rattle itself to bits, but she let Aiden work out his rage.

He took a sharp corner into a strip mall entrance, slamming her toward the parking brake, then against the door. Finally he pulled into a space in front of a tawdry row of shops dominated by a dollar bargain store with lurid Day-Glo posters plastered across its windows.

"That was some ride," Vivian said.

Aiden glanced over, embarrassment in his eyes. "I'm sorry."

"So what's the story?" Vivian asked, trying to sound casual, giving him permission to lie if that made him feel safe.

"My parents want me to see a shrink."

Vivian's eyebrows rose. "Oh?"

"They think I'm weird."

"My dear," she said, reaching over to squeeze his knee. "They haven't *seen* weird."

He smiled and covered her hand with his. "Thanks."

Vivian hadn't realized how tense his anger had made her until she'd unclenched at the sight of his smile.

"So, how weird do they think you are?" she asked, wiping a drop of sweat from her nose.

"They think I'm a Satanist."

"A what?" Vivian was amused.

"A Satanist. Just because I'm interested in the unknown. I mean, how would anyone learn anything if they weren't curious? How would scientists make discoveries? They're so narrow-minded. They're pissed off because I'm different from them. We all have the right to be different, don't we?"

Vivian nodded in sympathy. But did he realize how different people could be; he who wrote of exchanging skin for a pelt of brindle luxury? Would he grant her the right to be different? "What brought this on?" she asked.

"My aunt sent them some stupid book about teenagers

listening to heavy metal records backwards and committing suicide. That and a pamphlet called 'Ten Signs Your Child Has Sold His Soul to the Devil.' "

Vivian burst out laughing before she could stop herself. "But that's ridiculous."

"I know. I don't even like heavy metal." Even Aiden couldn't suppress a laugh now. "You always make me feel better, Vivian. You never judge me. You accept me."

Vivian wound her fingers into the hair at his temples and pulled his lips toward hers. "Yes," she whispered the moment before their lips met. When would he realize how far she would accept him?

Her claws, unbidden, traced promises on his back. The hothouse heat of the car made his body wonderfully pungent. She wished they were somewhere, anywhere, besides the front seat of his car. Should she wait for him to suggest they find somewhere secluded? *To hell with waiting,* she decided. *I'll take him down to the river.*

"Aren't you coming in?" a voice asked.

Aiden pulled away abruptly, and Vivian looked up to see Kelly peering in the driver's-side window.

"Uh, oh yeah, Kelly, in a minute," Aiden said.

"Where?" Vivian asked, not bothering to conceal her irritation.

"For pizza, of course," Kelly answered. She gestured to Mama Lucia's Pizza right in front of their parking space. Her smile was too sweet.

Vivian stared balefully over Aiden's shoulder. She knew Aiden would be too embarrassed to leave now. *I may kill you for this,* she thought at Kelly.

Kelly must have read her thoughts. She backed away from the car. "Coming?"

"Guess we better go in," Aiden said reluctantly.

Inside, a subset of the Amoeba sat around two tables dragged together under a ceiling fan that barely moved the thick air.

"Hey, Vivian," Jem said. Vivian decided his haircut wasn't so bad once you got used to it.

Others called their greetings, and Bingo toasted Vivian with her Coke.

"Wow, Vivian! Still beautiful!" Peter Quincey exclaimed as if surprised, and the girl who hung on him hit him in the arm.

The gang talked about videos while they ate, and Aiden and Quince argued amiably over something that had happened years ago in grade school. Aiden's left thigh pressed tightly against her right, and she yearned to be alone with him. She piled her hair on top of her head, hoping to catch a breeze on her neck from the fan. There was no relief from the heat. She thought again about the riverbank, but realized now what a stupid idea that had been. She couldn't be sure the Five wouldn't be prowling there.

They hung around outside the pizza place after they'd eaten while they discussed what movie they might go and see. The sky in the west was an angry red, and the heat wouldn't leave with the night. An air-conditioned theater sounded good to Vivian. She would find them a nice dark corner.

A motorcycle roared down the access road and came to a stop in front of the automotive parts store down the strip. She recognized it at once. Gabriel, helmetless, clad in jeans and tank top, silenced the growling machine.

He saw her, raised his eyebrows slightly, and stayed seated, staring at her with an inscrutable look on his face.

So what! she told him silently and turned away.

"What do you think, Vivian?" Aiden asked. "Killer death robots or sloppy love story?"

Before she could answer she saw a look of apprehension slide over Kelly's face, and Jem took a step back. Firm hands descended on Vivian's shoulders.

"Gabriel," she said without turning.

"Hi, babe," came his rumbling voice from somewhere above her head.

Aiden looked annoyed and hurt at the same time.

"A friend of my mother's," she told him, then, "Get your hands off me," to Gabriel.

His hands tightened on her shoulders instead, and she felt his breath on her cheek as he bent his head closer. "Let him go," he whispered in her ear. Then the pressure of his hands was gone.

She turned to see him strolling toward the parts store. *How dare he?*

There was a moment's silence; then Bingo hummed her appreciation. "Ummm-mmm. Buns of steel, absolutely."

"Who was that?" one of the gigglers asked breathlessly.

"A jerk," Vivian said, putting her arm around Aiden.

"He hasn't been bothering you, has he?" Quince asked, making a fist.

Vivian was touched by his concern. "No, he just irritates me," she said. Quince wouldn't last a second against Gabriel.

Aiden squeezed Quince's arm and shook him affectionately. "Come on, you guys," he said. "We've got a movie to see."

14

When Aiden called the next night he had bad news. "Don't tell anyone," he begged. "They'll never let me live it down. Guys don't get grounded."

Oh, yeah, Vivian thought. *Like, who am I going to tell?* She didn't imagine she'd see the Amoeba without Aiden to take her out with them. "How long?" she asked.

"Until I can get my mother to tell my dad to lay off."

How can he allow them to restrict him like that? Vivian thought. *What was wrong with him?* No one could cage *her* up. "That's awful," she said. "What are you going to do?"

"Paint my room, supposedly," he answered. "Dad's stacked a pyramid of cans outside my door. He said twenty-five coats should do it."

"What about work?"

"Oh, he's got that timed." Aiden's voice was brittle. "I can go to work but if I come home five minutes late he's phoning the courts to have me officially declared an uncontrollable minor."

Vivian wasn't sure what he meant, but the threat sounded terrible. "Can he do that?"

"God knows, Viv, but I don't feel like testing him. I thought he'd lighten up when he retired from the army. Fat chance. Sometimes I wonder if he wasn't blown up in Vietnam before I was born and they sent home a robot replica."

Vivian chuckled. "That would make you a cyborg."

"Huh?"

"Half human, half robot."

Aiden let out a delighted yelp of laughter, but it was cut short by someone calling out to him in the distance. "Gotta go. Parents home," he said, and Vivian found herself holding a dead line.

Vivian was surprised when Bingo showed up at her door that evening.

"Thought you might like some company since your boyfriend's in the slammer," Bingo said.

"How did you know?" Vivian asked.

"I phoned up to see what was on for the night and his old man told me," Bingo replied. "Well, actually," she continued, "what he said was, 'He's not spending any time with you weirdos until he cleans up his act.' "

Vivian laughed. She recognized the tone of voice. "Want to come in?" Thank goodness Esmé was at work. She could trust Rudy to be a gentleman.

Bingo poked her head through the door and looked around. "Neat house, but I got Jem in the car and a stack of videos. Wanna come to my place and OD on popcorn?"

Vivian hesitated. She wouldn't have Aiden to hide behind. What if she didn't know how to join in? What if she made a fool of herself? *But this is what you wanted, you coward*, she told herself. She ignored the flutter in her stomach and nodded. "Yeah. Thanks. I'd love to."

"There, I told Jem you'd come," Bingo said triumphantly.

Vivian wondered why Jem had thought she wouldn't. "Let me grab my bag," she said.

Bingo's parents were home, which explained why the entire Amoeba hadn't descended. "I told them it was their duty to go out so I could throw wild parties, but they wouldn't listen," Bingo said as she led the way upstairs to a small room that had been turned into a den for her use.

"Bingo's lair," said Jem, snapping his skinny fingers.

"Mom said she understood my need for privacy, but she was damned if I was going to entertain boys in my bedroom," Bingo explained as she flopped onto an overstuffed couch. "Put that one in," she ordered, jabbing a video at Jem, who almost dropped the popcorn but obeyed slavishly. "As if I couldn't do the same things she worried about in here," she said to Vivian, and winked.

Vivian began to think she needn't worry about keeping up her end of the conversation, but what did Jem feel about her coming along? It soon became clear, however, that Bingo and Jem were merely buddies.

The movie was wonderful — a real grade-B, drive-in clunker — and Bingo and Jem immediately began a sarcastic commentary on what was happening. "Hey, man, I'm having a bad hair day," Jem said in a falsetto as a zombie with clumps of hair missing shambled across the screen.

"I may be the president of the Hair Club for Zombies," Bingo added, parodying a well-known TV commercial.

"But I'm also a client," Jem and Vivian chimed in together.

The three of them fell about laughing.

"Your life is a bad hair day," Bingo said to Jem, and they screamed with laughter again. Vivian had to wipe tears from her eyes.

"You're all right, girl," Bingo said, and a flood of warmth surged through Vivian.

Halfway through the movie the phone rang. Bingo paused the tape and grabbed the receiver. "Yeah? Oh, hi, Kelly."

Vivian stiffened.

"Oh, hangin' out movie bingeing," Bingo said. "Yeah? No. Did they? Yeah, I heard. Phoned his house. Yeah, again. His dad's a real prick."

It was obvious the subject was Aiden. Vivian picked up one of the cassettes and tried to look as if she wasn't listening, but Bingo's next words made her glance over anyway.

"Well, why don't you ask her, Kelly? She's sitting right next to me." Her tone was mockingly sweet. "Bye-ee," Bingo sang in response to whatever Kelly said at the other end of the line, and she hung up.

"That girl can be such a bitch," Bingo said.

"What did she say?" Jem asked. Vivian never would have. She waited for Bingo's answer warily.

Bingo flung a hand up as if dismissing Kelly's words. "She was like, 'I guess Vivian won't be going out this weekend,' only she sounded happy about it, you know? She thinks you don't have any friends or something."

"She's jealous," Jem said, reaching for the remote.

"Oh, duh!" Bingo responded, then to Vivian, "She was like that to me before you came along, you know. I've been friends with Aiden forever, only when Ms. Me-First decided to claim him, suddenly I was the enemy, and I wasn't even competing."

"Let's watch the movie," Jem said.

"Aiden's too sweet," Bingo continued, ignoring Jem. "He was falling right into a thing with her, just 'cus it was easier than saying no and hurting her feelings."

"She's not that bad," Jem said, starting the movie again.

"Guys," Bingo said. "They think with this." She grabbed her crotch.

Jem laughed. "You're crude."

Bingo blew a raspberry at him. "Yeah, you love it."

On the screen a scientist put the severed head of a zombie in a pan and poured in a nutrient to sustain it. The zombie's lips wriggled and its eyes rolled.

"Mmmmmm! Zombie Helper," Jem said. "Pop it in the oven and bake."

Bingo added her own interpretation. "Now, baby, use your zombie litter."

"Good one," Jem conceded joyfully.

Vivian settled back into the cushions. This was great. She had an ally. Who would have guessed? She was having the most fun she'd had with anyone in ages, and they weren't even pack. *We can be friends,* she thought. *It needn't be them and us.*

But what if they saw her in her wolf-shape? They'd be fleeing down the streets like those teenagers on the television.

"Stop, wait," she said for a zombie that chased some kids down an alley. "Let's play Scrabble."

Jem and Bingo cracked up.

15

The trees in Gaskill State Park were festooned with crystal raindrops, and thunder still rumbled in distant skies. The air was thick with mist as the heat of the day steamed from the turf into the pewter light of dusk.

Figures wound through the trees and emerged into the clearing—pairs, singles, groups. Vivian watched them arrive from the fallen elm where she perched. Some chattered in hushed, excited tones, others came silently. Most had walked a long distance after the two-hour drive, their cars, vans, or bikes parked along lonely country roads, in hidden clearings and forgotten lanes—anywhere they wouldn't attract a park ranger's eye.

Lucien Dafoe hobbled between two friends, complaining loudly that he was still too hurt to fight. Vivian sniffed in disgust. Her people healed faster than that.

"I hope someone beats the crap out of *him*," Lucien said, nodding toward Gabriel, who was laughing with a friend. "Someone not so prissy about where and what he can hunt."

Gabriel pulled off his T-shirt and tossed it on the ground. His body was a sculptured, oiled machine straight out of an action movie poster. Vivian caught the smell of his musk on the moist, hot air — the odor of power and excitement mixed with that of cheap strong soap. It made the light fur on the back of her neck bristle.

Over by honeysuckle-strangled bushes stood Willem, Finn, Gregory, and Ulf. Ulf stared beyond his companions, ignoring their cackles and good-humored punches. His thin shoulders were rigid, his fists tight balls at his sides. Vivian followed his gaze and saw two figures entangled in the shadows of a white oak. If logic hadn't told her otherwise she would have thought they devoured each other. The female broke away, laughing, and left the male behind, clutching after her. She stepped into the clearing and revealed herself as Astrid. It was Rafe who pursued her, his mouth still open and wet from her tongue.

Rafe and Astrid! Vivian glanced back at Ulf and understood the taut fury on his face. *The slut,* Vivian thought. She didn't care who she hurt. Ulf now, Rafe later, if she won the bitches' match after the male Ordeal, and earned the right to claim the new leader as her mate.

"Did you see that?" Esmé sat down on the log beside Vivian and nodded in the direction of Astrid.

"Yeah," Vivian answered. "She's old enough to be his mother."

Esmé's lips twitched; then she tried to look serious. "God, Mom, you don't approve, do you?"

Esmé grimaced. "No. It can only lead to trouble." She paused, the smile returning. "Most of us only fantasize about it."

"Mom!"

Vivian didn't have a chance to continue. Renata strode up. Her shorts were unzipped and a fluff of tan fur already covered her belly. "Astrid's gonna cause blood between those young dogs one day." She wiped the sweat off her upper lip with a hand that tapered into long, long claws. "I'll kill that alley cat if she harms my son."

"Don't worry, Rennie," Esmé comforted. "Gregory's the most sensible of those fools."

Vivian sniffed. "That's not saying much."

Esmé dug her with an elbow and Vivian shut up.

"So," said Renata to Vivian. "Will you dance the bitches' dance? You're old enough now."

"No," Vivian snapped. She wasn't about to make an exhibition of herself to win the favor of whichever muscle-bound cretin won.

Esmé laughed. "She wouldn't want to hurt her old mom, would you, sweetheart? She's gonna cheer me on."

Fat chance, Vivian thought. *More likely die of embarrassment.*

A hum of interest buzzed around the clearing. With the first pale glimmer of moonlight over the tops of the trees, Orlando Griffin arrived and Rudy with him. They would act as referees this night, to see that the Law was carried out. The pack drew in and gathered around them to wait for Orlando's word. Vivian, Esmé, and Renata joined the others.

Vivian noticed some strange faces. Word of an Ordeal spread, Rudy had told her. Some lone wolves always showed up. One was a big, evil-looking blond with a scar on his cheek. She wondered if he was strong enough to take Gabriel.

The blond's slender male companion seemed more interested in catching Esmé's eye than sizing up the competition. He had a cheeky smile and Esmé made a warm throaty sound of interest. When she didn't turn her back on him, he came over and introduced himself as Tomas. He laughingly told Esmé to "get real" when she asked if he was going to join in.

"I'm too fond of my skinny ass to risk it fighting those brutes," he said. "I don't want to lead a pack. I prefer to hunt alone. Exceptions can be made, however," he added, winking at Esmé.

"The nerve," Esmé said after he left to talk to Orlando about helping referee, but she wriggled with pleasure.

Orlando raised his arms and the last whispers died away. "I will recite the Law," he said.

"When a leader dies by the teeth of a wolf, then the challenger leads the pack. When a leader dies by the teeth of fate then Ordeal is called, for only the swift and strong may lead. All willing adults may stand and fight, and fight they will while they stand. But when the first drop of his blood is shed, a fighter must stand aside. The final pair may fight to the death if neither will yield till he's died. So speaks the Law.

"Brothers, pay your respects to the Moon."

The males began to separate from the crowd,

shrugging off shirts, undoing flies, but their migration was halted by another voice.

"And sisters," Astrid said. She marched up to Orlando, and Vivian was outraged and delighted at the same time.

"You are mistaken," Orlando said politely.

"I am *not* mistaken," she insisted. "Recite the Law again, old man. All willing *adults* may stand and fight. Where does it say females are excluded?"

"It is tradition," Orlando growled, and the power of his youth burned in his eyes. "*No* female will fight. This isn't a game, Astrid. First blood can also be life's blood, especially when your opponent is twice your size."

Astrid puffed herself up indignantly, preparing to spit out her next argument, but Vivian never found out what it was because Gabriel spoke.

"Let her."

"What?" Vivian gasped, in concert with the murmur of astonishment that rose all around.

Orlando's jaw dropped in surprise, and a smirk of triumph made Astrid's face look evil.

"She's right," Gabriel explained. "The word of the Law does not eliminate females, though tradition has for good reason. But the bold Miss Astrid is welcome to a practical demonstration why."

Vivian could see the fight on Astrid's face between pride in being named bold and anger at Gabriel's dismissal. "She doesn't stand a chance of winning," Vivian said to her mother quietly. "Why's she doing this?"

"I bet I can guess," whispered Esmé. "She thinks if she can knock out some males, she'll already have a lead over us. That it'll be a much more impressive show of strength than beating up some weak little bitches."

Gabriel gazed steadily at Orlando, waiting for his decision.

Orlando finally spoke. "Does anyone object?"

People looked at each other, but no one answered.

Orlando shook his head as if with regret. "So be it," he said.

There was a disturbance on the other side of the circle from Vivian. Rafe pushed through, the rest of the Five behind him. "What about us then?"

Orlando's expression grew thunderous. "Will you dispute the word *adult* now?" he asked.

"Yeah," Rafe answered, sticking his thumbs in his belt.

Ulf's eyes flickered around the circle nervously; the other boys glared defiance.

"Having a hard-on doesn't make you an adult, boy," Gabriel said, and some of the grown males laughed.

Orlando waved them quiet. "The Law is specific in this matter, Rafael. Bone and flesh, flesh and bone, a man takes time to grow them. Two-five-two number the moons that it takes for a man to know them. Till then he is not the match of a man, and a man is not bound to match him."

"That's twenty-one years for you slow students," Bucky pointed out. Finn gave him the finger.

"How do I know you didn't make that up?" Rafe said to Orlando.

A collective growl went up around the circle. Ulf cringed.

"The voice of the Law never lies," someone shouted.

"Give it up," someone else called, and others took up the cry until Orlando raised his arms again.

Sharp, silver light etched the old man's wrinkled face into a craggy landscape as ancient as the moon's itself. "This is the Law," he said in a voice that was the Law. "You will obey or die."

The males moved silently through the crowd toward the Five, encircling them. Ulf looked this way and that, his teeth bared in panic. The smirks left the faces of Gregory and Finn. Then Vivian could see no more, for wide backs and shoulders obscured her view.

"Come on, Rafe," she heard Gregory's voice plead. "Another time, okay?"

"Yeah," Willem joined in. "We'll get other chances."

There was silence for a minute.

Finally Vivian heard Rafe speak. "Fuck you." It was a curse of defeat.

The tight wall of males relaxed, and Vivian caught a glimpse of the Five slouching through the crowd.

Gabriel slapped Bucky on the back and said something that made him laugh. The men turned to leave the circle as if this was a cue. Bucky passed the joke on to another. As Raul passed his wife, Magda, he grabbed her and kissed her deeply. A squeal caused Vivian to turn to her right and see Rolf and Renata in a similar embrace. Esmé stared at the ground, and Vivian knew she longed for someone to kiss for luck.

"Come on," Vivian whispered, tugging at her mother's T-shirt.

When they reached the edge of the clearing, Esmé

pulled her shirt over her head. Vivian took off her own blouse and slid off her shorts. In no time they were both as naked as the others who gathered in a semi-circle facing the clearing.

The combatants lined up in the center of the clearing, their backs to the watching crowd, their faces to the rising moon. Astrid, standing at the end of the row, looked absurdly small beside the others, like a child mimicking her elders. There were seventeen males in line, and some of them were anonymous from behind. There was no mistaking Gabriel, however. He was half a head taller than the tallest of them, and only the blond newcomer matched the width of his shoulders.

Esmé was playing who's who. "That's Jean next to Raul," she said to Renata. "I'd recognize that tight little butt anywhere."

Renata choked back a laugh. "Shhh!"

For a moment only the creaking and chirping of insects filled the air.

Then a rustling began in the woods across the clearing, beneath the rising moon. Closer and closer it came, and with it groaning. A pale figure took form in the darkness, and out stepped Persia Devereux dressed in silver robes. In her hands she carried a silver bowl, as ripe and as full as the moon. She sang a moaning soft song that throbbed like the heart of a beast. Aunt Persia was far away, but the music thrummed in Vivian's ears. She swayed to it.

The old woman offered each fighter the bowl. "Drink of the Moon," she said. And as she passed down the line, backs furred, limbs twisted, ears sprouted tufts. Vivian felt an answering crunch in her spine—sharp pain, sweet pain—and a warm rush of blood in her veins that swept to her hands and feet, causing her nails to pop and grow.

Aunt Persia reached Astrid the last. The lone female was already foxy red and, though she still had fingers to steady it, she lapped from the dish with her muzzle like an Egyptian god feeding. As Astrid lifted her head, a pearl of liquid suspended on her black lip, Aunt Persia cried out a guttural word in an ancient tongue and tossed the bowl over her head.

Vivian howled the answering word she had learned as a cub and fell to all fours.

She expected the center to burst, but the males stepped back as if they danced to a well-known tune, and Gabriel shot down the line, his legs evolving. He curled out a lengthening arm and swiped once, twice. "First blood," he boomed in hollow tones from the echoing cavity of his changing mouth.

Astrid reeled and her snout, dripping red, curled back to a woman's face with the shock. "Cheat!" she screamed with human lips, then made the full change and went for his throat. He tossed her aside like a rag.

Rudy and the skinny stranger, unchanged, ran to retrieve her and tried to drag her from the field of combat. She escaped their grip, tearing Rudy's side. Another male jumped her and she ripped his throat, sending him yelping back in surprise. The other males stared as she growled a challenge, unsure of what to do, until Gabriel grabbed her and threw her once more to the ground, and whatever he screamed in her ear as he pinned her made her collapse. He got up and stood over her, showing his canine long teeth, until she rolled onto her back to present her belly, eyes narrow with rage. When he retreated a few paces, she flipped over and slunk to the edge of the clearing several yards down from where the other females stood.

Vivian, like the rest, growled as she watched Astrid go. She knew if Astrid set one paw wrong they would all be on her. Astrid knew, too. She sank down to lie with her nose on her paws, but a ridge of fur down her spine still bristled.

A howl rose into the night.

Vivian pivoted to see an ancient grizzled wolf-creature keen at the moon, a pile of silver robes at her feet.

The males, all in their fur, answered—deep and baying.

Then the clearing erupted in a seething, snarling mass of fur.

16

Four males were eliminated before Vivian could blink twice. Spat out of the fur maelstrom, they staggered their separate zigzag routes to the sidelines with bloody flanks. One dragged a damaged leg. Another burst from the rumble and fled into the woods, tail between his legs.

Rudy and Tomas, still only partly changed, dove in to drag a brindle stranger out from under scuffling claws. The stranger lay motionless under the bushes, but he stayed in his fur, so he was still alive.

The remainder wove an intricate Celtic knot. The object was to wound and not be touched. To be wounded was to be disqualified. Jaws snapped, paws danced, bodies lunged, then rolled aside.

Vivian noticed the brothers, Raul and Rolf, on opposite sides of the fray. They would avoid each other if they could. Bucky had no such qualms about the two buddies he usually hung with. He feinted at one, then veered and sank his teeth into the other's throat. Gabriel took the first one by surprise when he ducked Bucky's feint, and ripped a hole in his shoulder; then

144

Gabriel turned his fangs back to the blond stranger, who retreated quickly.

Bucky brought his opponent down. They rolled, a growling mass of fur and spume, but Bucky kept his grip, forcing his teeth through the thick pelt. He must have tasted blood, because he released his hold, scrambled to all fours, and raised his muzzle in a brief triumphant howl. Vivian found she was howling, too. She choked it off in surprise.

Bucky spun around to protect his back. It wasn't wise to savor victory long. His defeated friend slunk toward the edge of the clearing, his belly close to the ground.

In the center, Gabriel and the blond stranger circled each other warily, their hackles spiked and their teeth bared. Rolf edged by them, intent on a gray who stood momentarily disengaged, his sides heaving.

That was a mistake.

The blond lunged, savaged Rolf's nose, and swung back to Gabriel in a snarling heartbeat.

Meanwhile, someone took out Raul; Vivian didn't know who, but she saw Jean lay low the gray, who had only made it this far from dumb luck.

Gabriel and the blond still circled stiff-legged. Their lips were wrinkled into masks of hatred; their sinews trembled with the stress of restraint. Gabriel struck, missed, tumbled, and was back on four feet before the blond's teeth clicked on air.

Bucky herded two other strangers like sheep. Jean joined him. They made short work of the unknown pair, and Vivian's heart thumped with the beauty of their fierce symmetry.

Then they had only each other to turn on.

They faced off, their jaws parted in laughter. Bucky glanced over at Gabriel and the blond, then back at Jean. He cocked his head and Vivian knew he said, "It's just us, buddy, unless you wanna come between *them*?"

Jean deliberately lifted his leg and sent a short stream of urine shooting in their direction. The message was clear: "Piss on that."

Vivian smiled at their banter, her mouth wide and toothy.

They broke apart, turned, gathered speed; they leaped and met in midair.

Bucky knocked Jean askew and landed straddling him. *Now for the quick nip,* Vivian thought, *and Jean is out.*

But Jean went for Bucky's throat. Bucky jerked away. He lost his footing and the laughter left his eyes. Jean tried to wriggle out from beneath while Bucky was off guard, but Bucky found Jean's belly under his chin. He buried his teeth in Jean's stomach. Jean screamed. It was either that sound or the smell of blood, but Bucky went crazy. He ripped and ripped and ripped, while Jean shrieked.

Vivian staggered with shock as Jean's entrails splattered the ground. *But they were laughing,* she thought. She looked around for someone to make Bucky stop, but these were all strangers about her, with froth on their lips and lolling tongues, lost in the kill, urging Bucky on. Their eyes stole the silver moon and turned it red. A chill shuddered through her, despite the hot, acrid air.

Gabriel and the blond circled the pair on the ground with their tails held high. The blond whined and made little nips with his teeth as if he longed to join in, but Gabriel twitched his nose at the smell of carnage and growled. It was his right to kill, his or the blond's, not Bucky's. He dragged Bucky off by the scruff of his neck and tossed him aside.

The blond lunged. He caught Bucky's throat in his jaws and shook him wildly. Vivian saw surprise in Bucky's eyes. *He's going to die,* she thought. But Gabriel jumped the blond from behind, and the blond let go with a yelp. Bucky fell over the body of Jean and sprawled on the blood-soaked earth. Jean shuddered into his human form. He twitched once, then lay still — motionless, ruined meat.

The blond turned on Gabriel, teeth bared. He wouldn't concede. No one had thought he would. There would be another death before the night was through.

They clashed in rolling, snarling fur, parted, then clashed again, the wounds opening wetly in their hides as if they were ripe fruit bursting. Vivian didn't care who won. She didn't want to watch but couldn't stop. Why did they have to make their beauty foul? What kind of people were they that they'd kill their friends? What kind of people invited strangers to a ritual death? Wasn't the joy of the run and the sweet, sweet night enough?

The end came suddenly, just when she thought the fight would go on forever while she burned to cinders from shame.

Gabriel grabbed a firm hold on the blond's thick ruff and leaped over his back, and the blond's head twisted impossibly. Vivian heard a crack. The blond's eyes bulged. He went limp. Gabriel let go, and the blond crashed to the ground, his head lolling. A dribble of blood ran from his lips. How easy it was, like killing a chicken for Sunday dinner. Revulsion squirmed like an eel in Vivian's gut and finally she could close her eyes.

She stood silently as the howls rose up around her, but she couldn't blot them out—Gabriel's thundering bay; Orlando's cracked, keening bell; the twining tenors of Rolf and Raul. The song was triumphant, hungry, impassioned. Her mother's soprano climbed to outrageous heights, and the young ones mimicked her, their reedy pipings swiftly turning hoarse. Even the Five were back, their voices lewd and raucous. The pack drew in close for the feel of fur on fur. The smell of sex was all around. Cubs would be fathered tonight. Vivian tucked her tail between her legs.

Then Esmé screamed and Vivian's eyes shot open.

Esmé twisted in circles like a puppy chasing her tail. She snapped at her back where Astrid straddled her, muzzle buried in Esmé's mane.

Vivian found her voice and yowled a complaint, searching face after face for a sign of help, but the others backed off and formed a ring. Rage surged through her. The fur stood on end down her spine and the backs of her legs. This was the female who'd mated their leader, had been a queen, and they let her be ambushed by that cheating red bitch. Astrid rode her like a rodeo bull and they didn't raise tooth or claw to help her.

Astrid shifted her grip and Esmé yelped.

In midair, Vivian wondered who had control of her body. She hit Astrid hard, but the red bitch kept her grip and brought Esmé down too. Vivian shook with a thunder from within. Were those snarls hers? All she could see was the muzzle gripping her mother's neck and Astrid's yellow eyes. Vivian went for the face.

Astrid's muzzle was streaked with blood. And still she held on. Vivian pushed between Astrid and Esmé to pry them apart. And still Astrid held on. Vivian clamped her jaws over Astrid's snout and kicked with her legs. And still Astrid held on, her yellow eyes mocking. Beneath them Esmé whimpered, then choked and gasped.

Her windpipe, Vivian thought. *It's closing up.*

Vivian wailed. She attacked the evil soul that threatened her mother—the evil that laughed with spite through yellow eyes. It took seven jabs to get the perfect angle: Six failed snaps glanced off protecting bone, then a canine tooth sank into a yielding surface, which held for a second, then popped like a yellow grape.

Astrid let go.

She rolled away, screaming as if to wake the dead.

Vivian didn't let up. She couldn't trust Astrid. What if the bitch was faking? She bulldozed hard into the whining female, and sure enough Astrid came up all teeth and claws. Astrid's fury did her no good. She wasn't as strong. She wasn't as fast. Vivian had never felt this much power before. It sang through her. She could tear the hide from the wolf in the moon, but she'd settle for Astrid's instead. She could bounce her, she could roll her, she could eat her inch by inch, and the growing terror in Astrid's remaining eye urged her on. She sliced a wound in Astrid's flank, herded her left and right, then circled her, making her dance a tight dizzy pirouette.

The red bitch gasped for breath, and the gooey mess on her face oozed black in the moonlight. She was weak, she had lost, Vivian wanted to kill her for that alone.

Around her, one by one, the pack took up a howl. It grew louder, and louder, till it crescendoed to the stars. Vivian shook her head. She wished they'd stop. Why did they have to make that racket now? She crouched to leap.

Then a body was in the way, then another, and another. She was within a circle of running female wolves. She twisted this way, that way, befuddled. They circled her as if they played a children's game— Aunt Persia, Jenny, Renata, Magda, Minerva, Odessa, Sybil, Flavia, more and more and more. She wanted to leap their heads and get to Astrid, but now she couldn't remember which way to go.

Then they were still.

Beyond them Vivian could see the males, standing as silently. All eyes were on her. *What do they want from me?* she thought, and dread slowly replaced the rage. She longed to flee, but was trapped in the thick, translucent night like a fly in amber.

I have done something terrible, she decided. *I have ruined the Ordeal.* Her heart constricted with fear. How did they punish that? But she raised her head and defied

150

them with her eyes. *I defended my own when you would not,* she thought. Yet the blood on her tongue tasted bitter. She was as bad as them. It was in her too—the thirst for blood, the need to kill. And where was Esmé, anyway? Dead on the sodden turf, no doubt. *Perhaps I deserve whatever they mete out as justice.* She stamped her front paws. *Do your worst,* she thought.

But bravado didn't stop her from cringeing when Aunt Persia stepped into the circle. The next thing that happened was baffling. Aunt Persia crouched on the ground, her ears laid flat. She rolled on her back and presented her belly. *What is she doing?* Vivian thought in shock. Then one by one the other females followed Persia's example, presenting their bellies, exposing their throats, paying tribute.

Oh, no. Oh, no. Vivian looked around in frantic confusion. Was this some nightmare? *It's not me,* she wanted to scream. *I am no queen.*

What had happened to ceremony? She'd thought the bitches' dance would start with some formal rite, not a sneak attack. She hadn't planned to be a part of it. But a female past her sixteenth birthday counted as grown. She crouched in horror and buried her nose between her paws.

This couldn't be right. No others had fought. What about the other females? Quickly she cataloged them—too old, too young, already mated, too fragile. She had never stopped to think before, she had been so determined to avoid the contest, but when no female strangers had arrived there had been only three possible contenders.

151

A soft tongue lapped at her nose, and with it drifted the sweet familiar breath that made her think of warm food and cozy beds. A muzzle nudged hers. She opened her eyes. Esmé. Safe. Dismay forgotten for a moment, she sprang to her feet and pranced a few excited steps.

But Esmé stepped aside, the circle parted, and toward Vivian, through the expectant pack, paced Gabriel, his sleek muscles rippling, his dark fur tipped by stars.

Vivian froze. Her happiness at her mother's safety drained away. She had accidentally named herself Gabriel's mate.

He stood before her, his jaws parted in a toothy grin.

She stared up into his ice blue eyes while he waited for her to admit his dominance.

A soft growl rose in her throat. *Never,* she thought. *You will not make me offer you my belly. I did not choose you knowingly.*

He grinned even wider at her defiance and licked his lips.

He would relish the challenge, would he? Well, to crown a queen you must catch her first.

She sprang past him down the aisle he'd already opened, along the tunnel of fur and out to the woods. She ran like the Wolf of the North made of stars in heaven, who with one long stride can leap over the top of Earth. The grasses she crushed made the night air pungent with freedom. But behind her she heard the thunder of Gabriel's pursuit.

17

Vivian climbed naked through her bedroom window and tumbled onto her bed. She had changed into her human form in the backyard bushes before she scaled the drainpipe to the porch roof. Only a rosy glow tinged the western sky. She hoped the neighbors weren't early risers.

It seemed an eternity since she'd run from the Ordeal. She must have flown like the wind to lose Gabriel, but she hadn't stopped to catch her breath until the sounds of his pursuit were long silent. She'd hidden in a shallow cave near a rocky crest until she was sure Gabriel hadn't tracked her; then she'd taken off for home. She'd never run that far before. The journey had taken all night.

Her palms and soles were bloody, and her body ached. Gingerly she limped to the bathroom and turned on the shower. She ran the water as hot as she could stand and drenched her body, her face, and her hair, as if trying to wash the last twelve hours away. *How could I do that to Astrid?* she asked herself over and over.

Esmé and Rudy hadn't come home yet, but they wouldn't be far behind her, she was sure. After the celebration, they would have stayed long enough to bury the dead in an isolated spot, then headed back. She cranked up the air conditioner in her other window and locked her door. How could they let her behave that way? How could they actually approve?

She pulled the sheet over her head, but she couldn't sleep. Was she truly obliged to become Gabriel's mate, or did winning the fight only give her first dibs, so to speak? Could she delegate the role? Maybe she could appoint Astrid. She giggled half hysterically.

Bloody Moon, why did Gabriel want her? Now he was pack leader, even some of the mated bitches would slink behind the bushes with him. He could go to one of the other communities and easily bring back a wife.

Vivian's eyes shot open with excitement. That was what she'd suggest. Surely the pack wouldn't condone his mating her against her will, would they? She relaxed and her eyes closed again. Sleep wound a cotton shroud around her.

When Vivian woke it was dark outside. The house was silent. She had slept the day away. She vaguely remembered half waking much earlier when someone rattled her doorknob. That must have been Esmé's voice she'd heard call her name. *I'll get up in a minute,* she told herself, then rolled over and tumbled back into unconsciousness.

The next time she opened her eyes, it was morning, and there was an insistent rapping on her bedroom door.

"What?" she called out angrily.

"Are you getting up?" Esmé asked.

"No."

"We've got to talk."

"No, we don't."

"Look, it's okay," Esmé said. "You're embarrassed about running away. Everyone understands. You were overwhelmed by what happened. You're young. You're used to boys. A man's a different matter entirely. But you're woman enough to handle him, I know you are, baby. You're *my* girl."

Boy, does she have hold of the wrong end of the rabbit, Vivian thought. *Don't bother telling me how Astrid is, and whether I've crippled her for life. Don't tell me how Bucky is coping with killing a buddy.*

"I didn't enter any competition on purpose, and I don't want Gabriel, so go to hell, Mom," she finally answered.

"Vivian!" Esmé sounded more hurt than angry.

The phone rang. "Okay, okay," Esmé said. "I'll leave you alone to get used to the idea." She left to answer the insistent jangling.

Vivian threw a glass across the room. It shattered on the window frame. Even her mother would gladly hand her over to a mate she didn't want.

All day Vivian came out of her room only when she was sure Esmé was elsewhere. She knew it drove her mother crazy. *Serves her right,* she thought. *If I hadn't had to save her ass, I wouldn't be in this fix.*

The phone rang constantly, it seemed. *Nosy bastards*, Vivian thought. *Don't they have their own sex lives to keep them busy?* She turned her television on loudly to drown out the ringing, but there were only stupid game shows on and a program in which fat women complained that their boyfriends couldn't accept them as they were. She turned the TV off in disgust.

Vivian stared at her unfinished mural of running wolf-kind, and the fine hair on the back of her neck bristled. She wondered if she had enough paint to obliterate it, but a pang of loss cut through her at the thought. *Nah*, she told herself. *That was the good times. The harmony. That's the stuff I want to remember.* An ache awoke for the blissful oblivion that seeped through her when she painted, and she went so far as to lift a brush from the jar on her desk, but the grip hurt her still-bruised fingers. *I'd have to go get water*, she realized. She tossed the brush down.

A squeak on the landing warned her Esmé was close again.

"That boy's on the phone," Esmé announced outside her door.

She means Aiden, Vivian guessed.

"Tell him I'm sick."

Esmé went away without arguing. *She'd just as soon put him off*, Vivian thought. *She only told me because she hoped the phone call would get me out of my room.*

After Esmé left for work, Vivian tried to phone Orlando Griffin and find out what her options were under pack Law. There was no answer. She slammed

156

the receiver down. Then Rudy came home, and she didn't want to call again with him around. She was relieved when he opted for an early night and left her alone with HBO. She fell asleep on the couch on purpose so she could snarl at Esmé when her mother woke her up to send her to bed.

Rudy rose early on Saturday to go bicycling before the temperature soared into the nineties, and Esmé slept in late as usual, so Vivian found herself alone when she wandered downstairs. She tried phoning Orlando, but again there was no answer.

"Where on earth has that old wolf got to?" Vivian muttered to herself. She thought old people stayed put and had routines.

The phone rang, and she answered before the bell had a chance to wake Esmé; then she cursed herself silently. What if it was Gabriel?

It wasn't. "Hi, Vivian. Feeling better?" Aiden had called again.

For a moment she felt out of sync with the world. His voice was so normal, so innocent.

"Not really," she lied. "I'm still kind of weak."

"Flu?"

"Yeah."

"That's a bitch," he said. "It's even worse getting sick in the summer."

"Yeah. Still grounded?" she asked.

"Yeah. But relief is in sight. My parents are going out tomorrow night. They're seeing old friends. People who keep them out late. Get it? Huh, huh? Wanna come over?"

"What about your sister?" Vivian asked. His sister seemed the type to squeal in a second.

"Going to a sleepover."

"That's convenient."

"You don't say. So how about it?"

She hesitated. The invitation was tempting in the extreme; any other time she wouldn't think twice, but with what she had done to Astrid did she dare let herself be alone with Aiden no matter how much she longed for him? She'd thought she was in control of herself; now she was no longer sure.

"Please, please, Viv. I miss you." Aiden's voice was hushed and seductive, as if his head lay on a pillow next to hers. Desire stirred in her. "I miss your toes," he continued, "I miss your feet, I miss your calves, I miss your knees, I miss your thighs, I miss your . . . intellect."

Vivian burst into laughter. How could that funny, sweet boy bring out the violence in her? He wasn't like Astrid. "Look, I'll call you tomorrow and let you know how I'm feeling," she said.

"Early, or I couldn't stand it."

"Early," she promised.

"Cool."

Vivian was still smiling when she walked into the living room, but what she saw there wiped the smile off her face.

"How did you get in?"

Gabriel lounged in an armchair. "Rudy." Even at rest he looked powerful, and she kept her distance. She noticed the white of a bandage under the hem of his shirt, and the shiny pink and white of new scars on his arms. She thought of the damage he could inflict and shivered.

Gabriel grinned lazily. "Don't be pissed off at him. I pulled rank."

Yeah, Vivian thought. *And I bet you loved doing it.* "What do you want?" she asked.

Gabriel raised his eyebrows. "I thought you knew."

"Well, you can't have it," Vivian snapped. "So go." Inside she was trembling. She marched out of the room and to the kitchen, where she banged the toaster oven open, then grabbed a bagel and began to saw at it with a serrated knife.

Gabriel came up behind her and placed his hands over hers, stilling her motions. The heat of him scorched her from the backs of her knees to the nape of her neck. "You're gonna cut yourself that way," he murmured, his breath in her hair.

"Who cares?" She thought briefly of slicing his hand but dismissed the idea. He was much bigger than her and didn't mind hitting females.

He took the bagel and knife from her, and she ducked under his arm and left the heat of him behind. He cut the bread carefully. "Toasted?" He was so damn calm, so irritating.

"No."

He placed the bagel in the open toaster oven and pressed the lever. "Sure."

She folded her arms across her chest and glared at him. "So. Are you going?"

"We can take it slow," he said. "You can learn to be

with me. Find out what I'm all about. You never know, you might like what you find."

"Don't hold your breath," she said.

He stepped toward her casually, amusement flickering around his lips. She tensed, her eyes checking for a way to run.

"Or . . ." His hand lashed out, grabbed her, and whipped her into his arms, where he held her tight. "We can take it fast and rough." His mouth came down on hers and his hot tongue parted her lips. She pulled back, but he caught her hair in his fist and pressed her close. She pushed on his chest and struggled in his arms, but he wouldn't let go. *Damn him*, she thought, tears forming. *I don't want fierce, I want gentle.*

When she tried to knee his groin, he pulled away of his own accord, laughter in his eyes.

"You think you're such a stud, don't you?" she said.

"Don't you?" he asked.

She stormed out of the kitchen to the dining room.

He followed her. "I see I'm required to court you in every room of the house."

"Not likely," she replied.

"I'm looking forward to the bedrooms," he said.

"Go to hell!"

His grin faded. "I *will* court you," he said. "And I won't give up. I will wait for you like I waited for you outside that cave, and I'll follow you like I followed you home that night, keeping you safe. I *will* wait for you because you are meant to be mine"—his voice grew husky with desire—"and because you'll be worth

160

the wait. Goodbye, Princess Wolf. Let me know what deeds must be done to win you."

When he'd left she could still smell him in the room as if he'd claimed her whole life.

"I'll choose my own mate," she swore, and walked to the phone.

18

"What if I were a magical creature?" Vivian asked Aiden. She could hear him breathing on the other end of the line. She wished her heartbeat were as slow and steady.

"What kind of magical creature?" he asked.

"What if I could change into something else?"

Aiden laughed. "Like a selkie in a Scottish fairy tale?"

"Or . . . like a wolf," she said.

"You'd be a very beautiful wolf," he said.

She smiled. "I am."

"And, Mademoiselle Wolf, what do you want from me?" he asked.

"I want you to think about what I've just said," she told him. "I'm coming to you tonight, and I'll make it true."

It was after nine, and the fat, lazy night hummed with the gossip of insects and wallowed in too much perfume. The heat of the day had yet to fade, and

Vivian plucked at the damp material of her dress as she crossed the main road and entered the tree-lined streets of Aiden's neighborhood.

Fear fluttered in her chest. She was defying pack Law. *But no one has to know,* she thought. *Just Aiden and me. What harm can there be in that?*

She knew Aiden thought she was playing on the phone that morning. She knew she would have to show him to make him believe. But if she had started him thinking about her changing form, that might help him accept it more easily when she finally did. She imagined the look of wonder on his face as she changed before his eyes. He might even be a little frightened at first, but he loved her, didn't he? She could see it in his eyes. He would know that she'd never mean him harm. He loved her and she loved him. She shivered with excitement. She had never put those feelings into words before. *I want to share my life with someone I care about,* she thought. *What gives them the right to tell me who to love?*

But what if the pack found out? Would she and Aiden have to run away together? Surely he'd want to when he found out she'd been claimed by another. He chafed under his father's rules. He wouldn't want to stay. They could go somewhere far away. They wouldn't starve. She could hunt for them both.

She laughed abruptly. She sounded like one of those romance novels Esmé consumed like popcorn. Aiden needed his parents to pay for college. She didn't want to ruin his life. But she did want someone who'd appreciate the sheer beauty of what she was. He would

163

understand why she didn't want to make light of life, or use her strength to lord it over others. He'd understand that being was enough.

Maybe there was even a way to change *him*. She'd never known it done, but there *were* legends—survive the bite of a werewolf and a human became one; drink water from the pawprint of a werewolf; smear on a magic salve—legends were often based on a nugget of truth. Oh, he would love that. She knew he would. He wanted so much to be special. But he wouldn't lord it over her, or soil his new ability with blood and power. He would be her true mate.

She walked up the flower-fringed path to Aiden's house. She paused to take a deep breath and speak a prayer to the Moon. The Moon looked after lovers. A bead of sweat trickled down the low neckline of the soft cotton sheath she wore. Her rat-a-tat knock echoed the beat of her racing heart.

"It's open," Aiden called from inside. "Count to ten, then come in." There were excitement and secrets in his voice. He echoed her mood as if he were her soul's twin. Her eagerness for him eclipsed her fears.

She was curious and impatient, but she indulged him. Slowly she counted, then tried the knob, and the front door opened easily. She stepped from the thick night heat into a shadowed hallway filled with cool, discrete air.

She didn't bother to search the first floor. He wouldn't be there. She understood his game. Instead, she quietly ascended the stairs. As she came closer to the landing the apple-sweet warmth of him filled her nostrils. She knew exactly where he was.

She approached his room languorously, enjoying the soft slide of cotton across her thighs. She was torturing herself as well as him, drawing out anticipation with excruciating delight. *To hell with telling him right away,* she thought. *Maybe I'll love him first.*

Hot steamy air that mimicked the night lingered outside an open door. She drifted inside and saw a bathroom, the tub still full. He didn't have to bathe for her. She would have devoured his sweat, licked it from him, and rubbed herself against his fragrant body until she became his essence. *No matter,* she thought. *I will make him sweat more.*

A delicious shudder went through her. She dropped to her knees by the tub, then lowered her head and lapped up a sip. The water tasted of him. *I'm coming to get you,* she thought delightedly.

She hummed the catchy refrain of a popular tune with wicked words as she neared his room. At his bedroom door she stopped. "Am I still cold?" she said aloud, and waited a moment. She reached for the knob. She thrust open the door. "Or am I hot?"

She let the door slide from her hand to thud gently against the wall and stood framed in the doorway. Her triumph transmuted to wonder as she saw the candles. A motley assortment of every shape, size, and color covered every spare surface. There had to be at least a hundred. They gleamed like stars and turned his room into a glittering grotto.

"Where did you get them all?" she asked breathlessly.

"Oh, I scrounged," Aiden said. He was in his bed and, apparently, naked under the sheets.

"I expect you need them to keep you warm," she said.

He blushed and looked away from her amused scrutiny, obviously wondering if he'd miscalculated.

She felt a familiar tightening of her spine. *The change?* she thought. *Now?* Her knees popped. Was the Goddess telling her not to waste time making love?

"It's a lovely way to be met," she said to Aiden, and her voice wavered. Aiden smiled despite his red face. He probably mistook the tremor in her words for sentiment. A ripple rode down the flesh of her back. "This is the perfect setting for the magic I was planning to show you tonight." But she had expected more time to prepare him.

His smile grew wider.

"You wanted magic, didn't you?" she asked, not expecting a reply. She was compelled, as if a full moon hung in the sky. "You wanted something special to happen, but you never thought it would. Well, I can show you what you've never seen before. Something beautiful, and wild, and beyond imagining."

His eyes half closed and his lips parted expectantly.

Vivian laughed. "No, silly. I want to show you what I can turn into." Excitement took over now that there was no turning back.

She kicked off her shoes, then took hold of her hem and lifted it, wriggling a little to bring the dress over her head. She tossed her dress aside and stood in only her panties.

Aiden let out a short breath more sigh than moan.

She slid her panties to her knees and let them slither down her calves. She stepped out of them and the blush of the change crept like an itching rash across her chest. Sweat trickled down her sides despite the chill air.

Aiden held his arms out to her. His breath grew harsh; his eyes burned with fever. She wanted to give in to his desire; that would be so much simpler than explanations; but her body had other plans. "Not yet," she said, and twitched. "When I change back. First I will show you my secret."

He frowned and opened his mouth to speak, but she hushed him.

"Remember your poem, 'Wolf Change'?" she asked. "This is your poem."

Her heart picked up speed. She flexed her hands as they filled with her hardening pads; stood on tiptoes as her soles roughened. But when she felt the first prickling of hair on her back she had a rush of doubt. What if he didn't love her in her wolf-skin? Was ancestral hate ingrained too deep in them all? She glanced outside to take strength from the high-flying three-quarter moon. No, he would see the beauty.

A jolt of painful ecstasy doubled her over, and her arms wrapped around her belly. Aiden sat upright in bed. "Are you okay?"

She grinned up at him through her tumbling hair. A

sharp tooth pricked her lip. "It's all right," she said. "Wait and see." Her voice held a throaty rasp.

A shivering tickle of hair grew over her shoulders and crept down her arms. Her elbows popped.

Aiden looked puzzled.

The change came fast then. Her arms lengthened, her legs shortened, her joints reformed. She uttered a guttural cry of pleasure as her spine extended into tail, the bone quickly wrapping itself with flesh, then fur. She felt the creaking, crunching as her jaw extended, and her eyes now saw the rainbows around each candle flame. She looked to see Aiden's amazement and pleasure.

Aiden's face was white in the flickering candlelight, his eyes large. He drew his limbs close to his body. Awkwardly he shifted away from her, crushing his back against the headboard. His mouth opened into a gash and from it came a hideous whining sound. Naked and wormlike, he cowered on the bed like a nightmare view of an asylum inmate. He stank of fear.

Her thudding heart grew cold in her expanding chest. She tried to reverse the change but her body wouldn't listen. "No," she called to him. "I mean you no harm." But the hand she held out in love grew claws.

He screamed.

"Wait," she said. "I know. I know. I look odd now but the end is gorgeous." But the words came out in a hollow growl from a mouth not meant to speak. Spittle flecked her muzzle with the effort.

As she completed the change, Aiden began to cry, silent tears coursing down his stricken face.

The bile of self-loathing rose in her. How could she be such a fool? Mixed with her disgust at herself was contempt for Aiden's cringeing, then guilt because she had caused it. Her heart broke for him because he feared, because he couldn't see the wonder, then raged at him because he made her feel unclean.

I came here for you to comfort me, she howled. *I thought you'd understand.* But she could tell from his face that all he saw was a savage beast. *I am not like them,* she cried.

He groped for the table beside the bed, his eyes on her face.

Look, I am lovely, she begged him. She whimpered and wagged her tail like a dog.

He flung a mug at her head.

No! she howled as it smashed on the wall behind her.

He hated her. He loathed her. She brought him pain. She didn't belong here. She didn't belong anywhere. She had to get away.

The quickest way out was the window. She didn't care what lay below. The last thing she remembered was a shattering, and she flew through the air amid glittering shards of glass.

19

Vivian woke with the coppery taste of blood in her mouth. She frowned and groaned, then opened her eyes. She closed them quickly when bright daylight sent a lightning stab of pain through her skull. Her head throbbed in the aftermath.

She was in her room, that was certain. She could tell she was naked and uncovered on her bed, the sheet twisted around her ankles, but she couldn't remember how she'd gotten there.

The air was thick with a stench too jumbled to separate and identify. It hurt to try. Why did her whole body ache? What did she do last night?

Aiden! She remembered the way he'd cringed from her. "Sweet Moon," she moaned.

But what next?

She had leaped from his window, she knew—it was a stupid, crazy thing to do—but the Moon looks after her own and she'd hit the ground running. And that was all she remembered—running, running, running.

Or was it? She thought she saw Rafe's face in there somewhere. Or was that a dream she'd had?

The room was filthy hot. She would love to turn on the air conditioner, but every nerve end cried out to her, "Don't move!" Ignoring the caution, she shifted slightly, and her stomach heaved. *Okay, okay, I'll just lie here,* she told herself. *The heat's not that bad.* Maybe if she was lucky she'd fall asleep again and wouldn't have to think or feel.

She wasn't lucky. She lay bitterly awake on the cusp of nausea as the events in Aiden's room replayed over and over within her head.

I'm so stupid, she thought. *So stupid. Stupid. Stupid.*

She tried to move past that moment and on to events beyond, but the night opened up like a black pit of nothing with no landmarks and looped her back to the scene in Aiden's room. Time had passed, that was all she knew, and a chunk of her life had been torn away while she'd been mobile and mindless and in despair. It was as if she hadn't existed for that time. Was that nothingness like the nothingness of death? She tried to imagine a forever of nonbeing with no conscious moments ever again. She shuddered despite the heat.

She had heard of this happening—a change coming on so violently that it wiped away the human side and the animal reigned supreme. That was in stories, though, and triggered by great passions like jealousy or rage. She'd never known it to happen to a real person. And— the nausea rose again unbidden by movement—usually something terrible happened during the blackout.

171

Stop being an asshole, she told herself. Obviously the stories were based on reality, but the terrible parts were there because they *were* stories.

She was sticky and gritty and dehydrated. *I need a shower,* she thought. She imagined floating in a bathtub full of water and ice. The image was so comforting she held on to it and almost lulled herself back to sleep, but it also woke a tortured thirst.

She opened her eyes again, slowly this time and only halfway, and peered through the slits. Her head still hurt, but if she moved carefully maybe she could stand the pain. Right now water from the bathroom tap promised to be sweeter than ambrosia. She smiled slightly at the thought, and something cracked and crumbled around her mouth. She raised her hand to her lips and found a rough crust there. She inspected her fingers and saw rust-colored flakes. A hollow thud increased its tempo within her.

I must have bitten my lip in the jump, she thought. *That's it. Or maybe I caught a rabbit. Yes.* And underneath, in the back of her mind, another voice cried, *Let it not be human.*

She sat up, ignoring the screaming pain that went with the action, and the cold sweat that ran down her back. She looked down and found she was streaked with the remnants of blood. The sheets were blotched with it, dry and brown amid the evidence of vomit. She could smell the blood clearly now amid the sweat, puke, and tears. It was unmistakable. It *was* human.

She heaved over the side of the bed and weakly grabbed a handful of sheet to wipe her mouth. "Oh,

172

sweet Moon. What have I done?" she moaned. Then a colder fear grabbed her. *Not Aiden?*

She scrambled off the bed, becoming entangled with the sheet, and barely missed treading in the pool of her vomit. At the door she realized—*I can't go to the phone like this. What if Esmé sees me?*

She grabbed her robe from the back of the door and fled to the bathroom, reaching the toilet bowl in time to throw up again.

Her shower wasn't the peaceful bath of her fantasy. She scrubbed her skin raw as she tried to erase even the ghost of a stain, and washed her hair till the roots hurt with the wringing. All the while tears streamed down her cheeks. *I couldn't have,* she told herself. *I wouldn't have hurt him, no matter how much he hurt me.* But she wasn't sure.

She approached the phone in the upstairs hallway swathed in towels.

"Is that you, hon?" Esmé called from her room.

"Yeah, Mom," Vivian answered reluctantly. The words came out as a croak.

"Are you sick?" Esmé asked.

In a big way, Vivian thought. "Yeah, Mom."

"Then go back to bed," Esmé answered, and ended the order with an inappropriate giggle.

Great Moon, she's got someone in there with her. For once this didn't annoy Vivian. At least that would keep Esmé out of the way.

Vivian picked up the phone, then panicked. *What do I say if his father answers? "Hi, this is Vivian, is Aiden dead?"* She swallowed a hysterical laugh and punched out his number. The receiver trembled in her hand, and the ringing shrieked through the soft tissues of her brain. It went on and on and on. *They're at the police station,* she thought. *Or the hospital. His father's identifying the body right now.*

Then someone answered. "Hello?" It was Aiden.

Vivian slammed down the phone. "Oh, thank you, thank you, thank you," she whispered to the Moon.

But if it wasn't Aiden's blood, whose was it?

She found a fresh pair of shorts and a clean T-shirt and got dressed, listening to a news station on the radio, but all she heard were endless baseball scores. After she'd mopped the floor with her towel, she bundled it up with her sheets and dragged the lot downstairs and threw everything in the washer. She switched on the local cable TV news and sat through reports of another shooting downtown, sexual harassment in the federal government, and some stupid boat show at the conference center.

Then, as she was trying to force some cereal down, a siren wailed through the streets close by, then another, and another. She pushed her bowl away and reached the door in time to see an ambulance tear by, followed by a motorcycle cop. She took off after them.

The midday heat seared her lungs as she ran, and the world was a white blast of sun. She could hear a dying siren up ahead and crackling radios. She turned right at Dobb's grocery to find Tooley's bar, on the corner of the next block, surrounded by a thousand flashing lights. It looked as if every cop from the surrounding three townships was there. Two fire engines rumbled like dragons waiting for lunch, and there was a rescue squad truck idling alongside the ambulance. A crowd was gathering.

She stumbled along the cracked, mossy sidewalk, gasping for air. Her hand trailed along the brick of the barbershop as if its roughness could summon reality as well as balance. When she reached the cross street, one of the fire engines let out a squeal and she flinched. It belched once, then pulled away. She saw that the remaining activity seemed to be centered around the back door of the bar, which opened onto a small yard containing a Dumpster.

As she reached the upholsterer's directly opposite the yard, a policewoman strung a plastic yellow streamer across the entrance. *Sweet Moon,* Vivian thought. *Is this my doing?* She turned away and pressed her forehead to the filthy shop window.

Behind her came a clatter of boot heels and a jingling of chains. She whirled to face the noise and saw the Five. The twins and Gregory almost danced, they were so full of electric excitement.

"Hell, Vivian. You look like shit," said Finn.

She flipped him off.

"Ooooh, she's sooo tough," Gregory responded.

Willem shoved him. "Leave her alone."

"Better not let Gabe know you're still sweet on her," Gregory told him.

"Yeah. He'll kick your ass," Finn said.

Willem spat at his twin. Finn dodged the wad.

Rafe hadn't spoken a word. He just stared at her with a look of smug amusement on his face. Ulf stood beside him fidgeting.

"What's happened here?" Vivian asked gruffly.

Ulf finally spoke. "They found a body behind the Dumpster." His voice was squeaky. "Some guy."

Vivian felt a cold lump in her gut.

"We didn't get to see it," Willem told her. "But there's a lot of blood."

"A goddamn river of it down to the drain," Gregory added with relish. "I heard some cop muttering about wild animals." He cackled with delight.

Across the street an ambulance took off quietly. One of the police cars followed. Lucien Dafoe came around the corner. That didn't surprise Vivian; Lucien was Tooley's best customer. He leaned against the door-jamb of the bar entrance and grinned at all the activity. He should have the sense to look shocked even if he didn't care.

Vivian realized then that Rafe had asked her a question. "What?"

Rafe folded his arms and cocked his head. "I said, did *you* see anything, Viv?"

"Huh?"

"Down here. Last night. I saw you in your wolf-skin under the bridge. You were heading this way."

The sun scorched her head, setting her skull on fire. Her tongue felt thick, and it was difficult to talk. "Was I?" She tried to sound nonchalant.

Rafe chuckled, but his eyes looked cold and eager.

"Got something to tell us, babe? Something we should know about? Huh?"

"You're full of shit, Rafe." She had to get away before the trembling inside broke loose. She couldn't let them see her panic. "There's nothing more to see here. I'm sure Esmé will fill me in on the details after her next shift." She turned to go.

"Don't think you're any better than us, Viv," Rafe called after her. "We saw what you did to Astrid."

She walked back the way she had come, in the knife-sharp, white summer heat, through a neighborhood as alien as the landscape of her dreams.

It wasn't me. It couldn't be me, she thought. But the blood she had scrubbed from under her nails proclaimed her a liar.

20

When Vivian woke on Sunday, the air in her room was cool and sweet, and the sunlight that stole between the curtains was pale and innocent. She could hear the radio playing softly downstairs. *It was all a dream,* she thought, and took a long, deep breath. Aiden still loved her. There had been no blood on her face.

The moment she entered the kitchen Vivian knew she'd been lying to herself again. There were dark circles under Esmé's eyes and her hair was haphazardly gathered back in a single comb. She was still in her nightgown. "Feeling better, baby?" Esmé asked vaguely, and stared into the distance as she sipped her coffee.

"What's wrong?" Vivian asked, dreading the answer.

"They found a body in back of Tooley's Saturday morning."

No one had told Esmé that she'd been at the scene, Vivian realized. "So?" she said, her heart thumping.

Esmé set her mug down. "The cook who found the

body described it to me," she answered. "Unless something's escaped from the zoo, the killer was one of us."

Vivian tried to look shocked. "Who would do that?"

"That's what we need to find out, because if this keeps on happening it'll be West Virginia all over again."

"But this is the city," Vivian said. "They'll think it's a psycho."

"Maybe the police and the newspapers will put it down to a psycho," Esmé answered. "But there's always someone who can put two and two together and come up with werewolf. And what if he fancies himself a hero?"

"Maybe it won't happen again." *I won't let it happen,* Vivian thought.

Esmé shook her head. "I'd like to think that, but it doesn't work that way."

Vivian fought down panic. "What do you mean?"

"Once someone goes over the edge and gets a taste, he can't seem to stop. It happened in New Orleans. That's why the pack moved to West Virginia years ago. And then it happened there, too. Your father said we could live in peace as long as we kept to ourselves. He was wrong. Now I wonder if we ever can have peace. The stories the humans tell say we're cursed. Maybe they're right."

Vivian's mouth was dry. She could hardly speak. "Even if the killer is seen, even if the killer is tracked and caught, they won't know there are others, will they?"

"I don't know, Vivian. I don't know where this will

lead. We're not invulnerable. You should know that after what you've seen."

Vivian hung on desperately to the way Esmé said "he" over and over; the word put a thankful distance between her and the body. She couldn't stand the shame if her mother knew. What if she'd brought death to her people, all because she'd thought a human could love her?

The doorbell rang.

"Bloody Moon," Esmé said, swiping at her hair. "That's Gabriel."

Vivian's voice caught in her throat. "What's he doing here?"

"Don't worry," Esmé snapped. "Not to court you, Miss Priss. He wants to know what I found out last night."

Then why didn't he ask you on the phone? Vivian thought. How could she face Gabriel, who always seemed to see right through her?

"Go let him in while I tidy up," Esmé ordered.

When Vivian opened the door she was relieved to see Rudy pulling into the driveway. Gabriel turned to greet him before she was obliged to speak. Rudy slapped Gabriel on the back and ushered him in.

She was going to disappear upstairs but Gabriel called her back. "You should be in on this, too."

What did he mean by that? Did he know something?

Esmé came downstairs wearing a short sundress. Even disaster didn't deter her where Gabriel was concerned. *Weren't you turning him over to me, Mom?* Vivian thought.

They settled in the living room, where Esmé described in detail the condition of the corpse. Vivian didn't want to hear, but she couldn't do anything to shut the words out. *I wouldn't do that,* she thought. *I couldn't.* But again she remembered the blood on her sheets.

"The people at the bar think the killer was a rabid dog or a big cat someone was keeping as a pet that got loose," Esmé said.

Vivian spoke up although she'd not meant to. "Maybe that's what the cops think." She remembered that Gregory had mentioned a policeman mumbling about wild animals.

"Their forensic specialists are going to be pretty confused when they try to identify any hair, saliva, or blood they might find," said Rudy. "And the size of any bite wound won't make sense."

"Is that good or bad?" Vivian wondered out loud.

"That might depend on whether it's an isolated incident," Gabriel answered. "The night Astrid led a run by the river," he said, pinning Vivian with his piercing, icy eyes. "Did they bring someone down?"

"No." The intensity of his gaze frightened her, and the word came out quick and defensive.

"No one I've talked to so far has heard of any other mysterious bodies appearing, either," Gabriel said. "So if it doesn't happen again, maybe we'll be all right. Maybe after a while, when they can't identify the killer, the police will write the incident off as a weird one-timer they can spook the rookies on night shift with. Meanwhile, I'm going to order that no one go out in their fur if possible. The police are going to be searching for a large animal."

Esmé looked as if she wanted to protest but didn't dare.

"What if it does happen again?" Rudy asked.

Gabriel scowled. "Our job is to not let it."

"We need to know who to stop, first," Rudy said. "Got any ideas?"

"A few," Gabriel answered.

"Astrid?" Esmé suggested.

Gabriel shrugged. "Right now she's got an all-night alibi, not that I place much faith in Rafe's word."

Esmé rolled her eyes. "Still cradle robbing, huh?"

"What about Rafe's father?" Rudy asked. "Lucien hangs out at Tooley's drinking his meals. He's always getting into fights with that biker Skull and his buddies."

Vivian remembered Lucien watching the police, grinning.

"No," Gabriel said. "A fight would be loud. Someone would have heard it. This had to be quick. He wasn't expecting death and never got the chance to scream."

Vivian tried to picture the kill, afraid that she would suddenly see herself there, but desperate for the truth. Could she bring down a total stranger in that way, without anger, without cause?

"I could understand if this were some harsh winter hundreds of years ago, and we were starving," Gabriel said, his eyes glittering with anger. "But this wasn't a kill for food, it was for pleasure—a pleasure that could condemn us all. I'll be watching; others will watch for me; and when I'm sure who's done this I'll make him pay."

His words struck Vivian with the strength of a blow, and for a moment she couldn't catch her breath.

Gabriel rose to his feet and paced the room. Vivian watched him with cold dread. His arms were powerful; they could snap a neck with one smack. His legs were long, and even through his jeans she could sense the muscle and sinew that would allow him to run down the swiftest prey. When he put on his pelt he was a massive, dark, merciless animal.

"I understand the urge to kill as much as any of us," he said fiercely, and Vivian believed him. "But it must be controlled. There's no wilderness to hide in anymore. We can't run in packs in the mountains where travelers go unmissed for months, there are no black forests that stretch on for days, and it's been many centuries since we ruled small kingdoms in the dark center of Europe as if we were gods. *Homo sapiens* is everywhere, they outnumber us, and *Homo lupus* must live beside them. As much as we might crave to, we cannot kill them. To do so endangers us." He paused. "Sometimes I think we have outlived our time."

He yearns for the old days, Vivian realized with chill fascination. She wondered if part of his anger at the killer was because he could not allow himself the same luxury. She recognized deep within herself the same red spark of desire for a time when instinct wasn't bound and the young Moon found it easy to forgive. She shuddered and looked away.

"I'm sorry this has frightened you," Gabriel said, and she realized he was standing at her chair, studying her. His eyes were gentler than they had been moments ago.

"What makes you think I'm frightened?" she said.

"Vivian, I can smell it on you." He reached down and lightly stroked her cheek with fingers that could easily crush her throat. She didn't dare pull back. "I'm sorry you lost your home in West Virginia. I'll find you another, and soon, I promise. I'll make you safe."

She almost laughed.

21

Vivian sprawled on the couch and allowed the tears to dry on her face. All she'd done for the last three days was haunt the living room, listening to the most miserable music she could find and tying herself up in knots. At night she locked herself in her room and comforted herself with chocolate. Her dreams were of the dark and of blood.

The CD ended, leaving her in harsh silence, allowing the same old thought to ring in her head. *How can he not love me?* She clutched the pentagram she still wore around her neck. No one had ever turned her away. Even Gabriel wanted her. And all she wanted was some pale, floppy-haired human with huge dark eyes who didn't want her.

She knew now that what she'd done was all a big mistake—a stupid, stupid mistake. She should have enjoyed him while she could and never let him know she was different. What if he did something foolish? What if something terrible happened because of her?

And worse, what had she done when she left his house?

"What's wrong?" Esmé said, coming home to find Vivian in exactly the same place she had been when Esmé had left. "That boy dump you?"

Vivian turned away. She couldn't deny it, but she didn't want to talk about it, either, because then she'd have to go through the effort of inventing a reason why. The truth, of course, was unrepeatable.

"The nerve of him," Esmé proclaimed, but she sounded relieved. "What an idiot! Couldn't he see how lucky he was? Men! They're jerks. No matter what the species. There weren't any phone calls for me?" she added anxiously.

Vivian shook her head.

"Oh, baby, I know you feel rotten," Esmé said. "But he's not worth the pain. It couldn't have lasted, you know that. You can do better. Much better. You could have Gabriel—someone you can be yourself with. You've had your taste of rebellion, now it's time to get real."

Vivian didn't have the energy to argue. She'd thought she could be herself with Aiden, and now he was afraid of her.

"I'll make some dinner," Esmé said. "I bet you haven't been eating. How about a beer?" She left for the kitchen.

Esmé never offered her beer. It was a bribe.

Beer made Vivian think of Tooley's. The death behind that bar had been in the news all weekend. Aiden *must* think it was Vivian who was responsible.

What if he told someone about her? She needed to talk to him and convince him the murder was nothing to do with her. She laughed bitterly. And maybe she could convince herself as well. But she kept on putting off the phone call; she couldn't bear the thought of what he might say.

In the middle of dinner the doorbell rang. Vivian inhaled sharply and hope fluttered in her chest, but before she found the sense to rise, Esmé bounded to her feet and went to answer the door. Vivian sat, her hands clenched around her knife and fork, unable to eat. When Esmé came back with Tomas, the new-comer from the Ordeal, Vivian felt as if she'd been kicked in the gut.

"I'm going out, baby," Esmé said. "You gonna be all right?"

"Sure," Vivian replied wanly.

After Esmé left she went to bed early. Sleep was her only escape.

By the next night she could stand it no longer; she waited until Esmé had left for Tooley's, then dialed Aiden's number. She hoped she could catch him before he went to work.

He answered.

"Aiden?"

He hung up.

She waited, a cold lump in her stomach. Maybe he'd regret hanging up on her and call her back. The phone didn't ring. Perhaps he was waiting for *her* to phone him so it wouldn't look as if he was too eager to give in. Perhaps he needed her to insist. She called again.

He answered.

"Aiden, please . . ."

He hung up again.

She called back, stabbing the buttons, barely seeing the numbers through the prickling blur in front of her eyes. A recorded message came on. She slammed the phone down and snatched up a dish and flung it against the wall. Paper clips went flying. The dish crashed to the floor and skidded down the hall. Hot tears stung her raw cheeks.

A slip of familiar paper fluttered down to the surface of the table—Bingo's number. Vivian must have left it by the phone when she'd called to thank Bingo for the night of movies and popcorn.

Of course, Vivian thought, and she wiped an arm across her eyes. *I'll call Bingo. She's good friends with Aiden. I'll tell her we've had a fight and he won't talk to me. She'll persuade him for me.* Vivian reached for the phone again.

"Bingo. Hi! It's Vivian."

"You've got your nerve talking to me." Bingo's voice was taut and angry. Her words left Vivian stunned.

"What?"

"You know damn well what," Bingo replied.

But Vivian didn't. "I don't understand."

"After what you did to Aiden."

Oh, Great Moon, he'd told her, Vivian thought. *How could he tell her?* And how could Bingo sound so matter-of-fact? Shouldn't she be afraid? "We had a fight," Vivian said, trying to get back to the scenario she'd invented, yet floundering in confusion over Bingo's attack.

188

"A fight! I'll say. Another one of your jealous rages. He told me about them. He was afraid to even look at another girl in case you went off on him. I was surprised when he told me. I thought you were more intelligent than that. It just goes to show I can't judge people at all."

"Jealous rages?" Vivian found herself repeating stupidly. What lies had Aiden invented?

"Don't act innocent with me," Bingo said. "I've known Aiden for years. I care about him. He usually tells me things. It pisses me off that I didn't even know it was going on. For Christ's sake, you even said *I* was trying to steal him from you. And after I went out of my way to be friends." Vivian could hear the hurt in Bingo's voice and knew she would never believe a denial.

"I love him, Bingo," she said wearily, knowing it was useless. "I did something to frighten him, that's why he told you what he did. I didn't mean to upset him. I would take it back if I could, but I can't. I only want to tell him how sorry I am and to make him understand. Please help me."

Vivian could hear the hiss as Bingo inhaled through her clenched teeth before she answered. "He understands perfectly well why you threw a chair through his window when he tried to break up with you," Bingo said. "You're a crazy, jealous, spiteful bitch, and he doesn't want to see you ever again. He's in even deeper shit with his father now. If you want to do something for Aiden, you can send his parents money for that window and then get the hell out of his life." She hung up.

Vivian replaced the receiver slowly and quietly, her knuckles white with the effort not to smash the phone to shards. For a moment she had thought she'd found a path to Aiden; now she discovered it blocked by an avalanche of lies.

So that's what he's telling them, she thought. *I'm a crazy bitch to be avoided. Now he can stop seeing me and keep his friends safe from me at the same time.*

Vivian ran to her room and threw herself on her bed. She clutched her pillow tightly to her hollow gut. He was so cruel. He didn't want her, so he'd made sure nobody would.

But he hadn't told anyone what she was. Did that mean he still cared a little or was he afraid no one would believe him? If there was another killing would he brave their disbelief? She needed to know his intentions. She needed to know how safe she was. And she needed to see him again, because she yearned for his arms around her.

Aiden's car was at the far end of the College City Shopping Center parking lot, by the wooded strip that separated the shops from the movie theater. Perfect. She could sit beneath the trees and watch his car and no one would notice. She could sit still for a long time if need be.

The scant last quarter of the moon wouldn't rise until past midnight, but Vega gleamed brilliantly in the southern sky, the only star bright enough to defy the parking lot lights. Vivian longed for the velvet country sky encrusted with stars. Under such a sky, all nights

190

were cool, all nights were joyous, all nights were forever. She made do with fireflies for stars and watched
the parking lot through motionless, mildewed leaves.

At ten many of the storefronts dimmed. Employees
left close behind the last customers, and the parking lot
emptied. At ten-thirty a timer turned off most of the
parking lot lights, and the strip where Vivian sat was
plunged into deeper shadow. The only bright spot left
was the undulating marquee lights of the video store,
alerting summer-school juniors that there was still time
to rent *Surf Nazis Must Die.*

At eleven the video store lights went off, and Vivian
eased into a crouch. Fifteen minutes passed before she
heard his footsteps along the tarmac. Even then, her
only movement was the twitching of her nostrils as she
took in his scent. He reached his car. His keys jingled.
She was in motion.

One arm slipped around his waist; a hand went over
his mouth. She yanked him back under the trees,
feeling him squeal against her palm as his feet left the
earth. She clutched his back tight against her breasts
and whispered into his ear, "I can run faster than you,
remember."

He trembled at her words, and the smell of his sweat
was pungent with fear. It saddened her to threaten
him, but she suspected this was the only way she could
make him stay. "I want us to talk," she said. "Promise
you won't run away or yell."

He nodded, jerking her hand up and down. For a
moment she enjoyed the feel of her thighs against his.
She gently licked his ear to show him she wouldn't

191

really damage him. He whimpered and it cut her to the quick. She released him.

He turned and stepped back from her arms. "What do you want?" he asked, and his voice was high, his face white.

"I want you to understand," she said. "I didn't mean to frighten you. I wanted to share what I was—what I am—and give you the magic you were always yearning for. What's so terrible about that?" She was dismayed to feel the tears come to her eyes. She had so desperately wanted to remain calm.

"And what the hell are you, Vivian?" he asked, a tremor in his words.

"I am *loup-garou*. I am *Volkodlak*. A metamorph."

"Is that the same as a werewolf?" He still didn't want to believe even though he had seen.

"Yes. Although what I turn into isn't actually a wolf, but it's close."

"And when you drew that pentagram in my hand you were making me your victim," he said.

"Don't be an idiot," she answered. "That was a joke."

He took another step backward. "Look, I won't tell anyone," he said. "I promise. Only let me go."

"Aren't you even curious about me?" she asked, amazed. "I thought you craved the mystical. You wanted the bizarre, remember? I thought you would grab what I am with both of your hands and eat me up."

"I don't want to know any more, Vivian. Please.

192

Let's leave it at that. You go your way. I'll go mine. Okay?"

"Aiden, I thought you cared for me. How can you send me away like that? I want to be with you. I want you to love me."

He at least had the decency to look ashamed. "But it's different now. I mean, how can I . . . I mean, every time I touch you I'll, I mean, I'll know . . ."

"Know what? That I have this wonderful ability to turn into a beautiful, strong, swift creature? That I am a Child of the Moon?" The revulsion on his face told her different.

"Vivian, did you kill that man the other night?" His words came out in a rush.

"Is that what you think? That I'll put on my fur and kill you?"

He hung his head and didn't answer.

She softened her voice and came close to him again. "Aiden, have I ever been anything but loving to you?" She saw him tense, but he didn't back away. That gave her hope. "Aiden, have I ever been anything but willing?" She stroked his chest with her fingers, and he raised his head to meet her eyes. "You don't want a tame girl, do you?"

"No!" He flinched back. "I can't. I'm sorry." And he did truly sound sorry.

"You don't trust me," she said, frustration making her angry. "Do you think I can't control my other self? Do you think my teeth will grow as I lose myself in your pleasure?"

"I want to trust you, Vivian," he said, sadness creeping into his voice, "but every time I think of kissing you I see that other face. All the time I think, 'What has that mouth done?' and I don't think I can ever kiss you again."

His words piled like cold stones inside her.

"You're a coward," Vivian said. "I thought you were different from the rest, open-minded, but you're just like those parents you despise. At the first sign of the unusual you run. You tell lies about me and make people hate me. You take away my friends. You're the monster, not me. I only wanted to love you."

She took the necklace he had given her from around her neck and hurled it at him. "Maybe you made me *your* victim."

His hand slapped to his chest and trapped the pendant as it slithered down his shirt.

"Go," she said fiercely.

He looked at her in surprise.

"Go now," she repeated. She didn't trust her rage.

"I'm sorry it had to end this way," he said as he backed slowly away. "I really am."

"You think it's ended?" she whispered as his car door closed. "Oh, no. You'll be seeing me."

AUGUST

Satyr's Moon

22

Vivian clung to a log in the clearing at the back of her house, as if she were an alligator motionless in a swamp. The sodden evening air of August enhanced the illusion, and the pattern of the bark became her pattern, as her flesh pressed into the wood. She curled her toes and savored the crunch as her nails bit gouges in the log. The odor of mold and damp moss intensified as she crushed the bark, until the air smelled like a cemetery. Motionless and silent once more, she allowed the creaking evening chorus to monopolize the woods with their see-saw, chirp-chirp, grind-grind, eternal white noise. She envied their cacophonous serenity.

A nearby rustle announced a predator's careful tread, and her eyes opened slightly. He walked discreetly but wasn't trying to conceal his approach. *How polite,* she thought. She sniffed the salty tang of a young male, often aroused. Overlaid was a comfortable intimate smell like a warm bed slept in, and the faint hint of baby powder and spearmint chewing gum. Willem.

He paused beside the log as if trying to decide whether to wake her.

She rolled and grabbed his legs. The momentum sent him tumbling. She bit his calf as he fell. He yelped. She threw herself on top of him, pinning his arms and leaning a knee with gentle menace into his groin.

"Vivie!" he pleaded. "I didn't mean nothin'. Vivie, let me up."

Maybe it was his use of her baby name, or maybe it was his soft bewildered eyes, but the heat of her anger dissolved, and she slid to one side, releasing him.

"Damn, Vivie, I thought you were gonna hurt me." He scrambled to his knees, one hand covering his crotch.

"What are you doing here?" she asked.

Willem wiped his nose with his fist and glanced at her sideways. His smile was the old, gentle smile. "I went into Tooley's, you know, so they could enjoy throwing me out, and your Mom cornered me. She said since I didn't have anything better to do I could get my ass over here and keep you company. Said you hadn't gone out in weeks." He raised his eyebrows and cocked his head in a way that would have made her laugh three million years ago. "Want me to beat him up for you?"

How dare she? Vivian thought. *Who gave her the right to broadcast my private business?* "I can do my own beating up, thanks," she told Willem coldly.

Willem grimaced. "Yeah. Silly me."

198

"Why aren't you with those other gangsters?" she asked.

Willem shrugged, a frown touching his face. He kicked at the log with one of his engineer boots. "Oh, Finn thinks he's hot shit—pushing us around 'cus Rafe's not there to slap him down. I mean, Rafe's bad enough, but at least he doesn't make us do dumb-ass stuff to prove he can make us do it. Greg doesn't like that either so they're always arguing, and you know Ulf—dumb little turd'll go along with anything. At least Finn isn't screwing his mother."

"Rafe's always off with Astrid?" Vivian asked.

"Yeah. At her place. Helping her 'recuperate.' He thinks the sun shines out of her ass. I don't get it." Willem shook his head. "I don't blame him for staying there, though. His dad's being weirder than ever."

They sat in silence for a while as the night darkened around them.

"We used to have fun, Viv, didn't we?" Willem said finally. "Now I wonder who's looking out for me besides me. Those older ones, all they do is talk. And Gabriel, who's he? Is he gonna make us do stupid shit like Finn does, just to show he's boss? You know what? I think you're the only person I trust. You're cool. You never let us talk you into doing stupid shit." Willem fell silent again.

Oh, yeah. I'm so cool, Vivian thought.

"You know who did that killing, Viv?" Willem said suddenly.

Vivian's stomach turned over.

"Nobody knows," he continued. "That weirds me out. One of us killing, and nobody knowing who. Killing used to be something we did together."

A faint breeze picked up and heat lightning patch-worked the sky. Willem sighed.

Vivian gently punched him in the ribs. "Get out of here. Tell Finn where to stick it. Stand up for yourself, asshole."

He grinned sheepishly. "Maybe I will."

"Well, go do it now," she said. "I need to be alone."

"Okay, okay." Willem got to his feet. He hesitated. "But you stand up for yourself, too, okay?"

"Yeah, sure."

Vivian walked down Lincoln Avenue toward the park. She was going to stop moping and stand up for herself, like Willem had said. There was a free concert this evening: six local bands hoping to draw new fans into the college bars up the road. The Amoeba would certainly be there, and Aiden with them. She'd been making life too easy for him; it was time to make him look at her and remember how beautiful she was; then maybe he'd realize what a fool he'd been for rejecting her.

She had brushed her tawny hair until it shone, and summer highlights made it shimmer with silver fire. Her cropped shirt revealed her flat, taut belly above her low-slung skirt. Her flesh was smooth, soft, and golden.

A sign on a telephone pole caught her eye; it was the

third one she'd passed. This time she stopped to read and discovered a message from the police, warning the public to avoid any large dogs they saw running loose. She snorted with amusement. She suddenly felt better than she had for days.

Vivian was walking under the raspberry sherbet froth of a crepe myrtle when she heard the growl of a motorcycle approaching. She expected it to scream past and was surprised when it slowed to a grumbling presence beside her. She glanced over to see Gabriel's black Harley pacing her. Gabriel's expression was dark and brooding and a streak of fear ripped through her. Then he grinned and cut the engine.

She stopped when his bike stopped, as if unable to control her movements.

He looked her up and down, the admiration clear on his face. "All alone, baby? I find that hard to believe."

"Then don't," she said. Why had he come to ruin her good mood?

He ignored her terse rudeness. "Rumor has it your boyfriend broke up with you."

"Does everyone know my business?" she snapped.

"What puzzles me," he continued, "is why?"

"That's nothing to do with you," she said, and began to walk again. Inside she quivered. *What was he getting at?*

Gabriel pushed his bike along beside her. "I mean, look at you. He must be out of his mind. Where would someone like him find another like you?"

Vivian walked faster.

Gabriel matched her pace.

"You'd have to work hard to put off a horny young guy like that."

Vivian turned on him, furious. "Go to hell!"

His eyes mocked her. "Was it something you said, perhaps?"

Vivian didn't know whether to scream or hit him. She was damned if he would see her cry. Even if he deserved an explanation, which he didn't, she could never tell him the truth. If he knew she was capable of betraying what she was to an outsider, then he might believe she was capable of other betrayals.

"Vivian." His eyes lost the mockery they had held a moment before. "If you ever want to talk, you may be surprised at what a good listener I can be." The dark purr of his voice was almost soothing. "If you're in a muddle, I'm good at untying knots," he said. "And if something comes up that . . ." He thought for a moment as if choosing his words. "That even you can't handle, I've got muscle to spare. No questions asked. Okay?"

She had never thought of him as kind, but for a moment she wanted to fling herself into his arms and tell him everything. The moment passed. That would be stupid. Right now he thought her a lovesick girl, that was all, and perhaps he was only taking advantage of her grief.

"Thanks for your concern," she said, and wished she could sound gentler.

"Want a ride?" he asked. "Going to the concert, right?"

She thought a second. "Yeah," she said as a sort of apology. Anyhow, it would do Aiden good if he saw her arrive with a suitor the other girls obviously found desirable.

As she threw a leg over the bike, she noticed the duffel strapped on the back. "Going somewhere?"

"Coming back," he answered. "I went to Pennsylvania. There's a pack up there. I wanted to find out if they'd had any rogue wolves there recently—a renegade out for human blood who might have run this way."

"Any luck?" She didn't expect him to say yes.

"Nah. I'm going down to Charleston tomorrow, to see what they have to say." He kicked the bike's engine into life. "If they hadn't scrubbed down that parking lot I might not have had to go through this," he yelled over the engine. "Maybe I could have picked up a scent."

Vivian silently thanked Tooley for his cleanliness. But what if that hadn't been her spoor in Tooley's parking lot? Life would have been miserable, but less complicated. Ah, but what if it had been? Vivian looked at Gabriel's powerful shoulders and shivered.

Gabriel pulled away from the curb, and Vivian steadied herself by lightly holding his waist above the dusty leather jacket he'd knotted around his hips. There was no softness to his midsection. If he had been any other male, she would have run her hands up his muscled back and explored the hardness of him; she would have pressed herself close and teased him. But this was Gabriel. He didn't behave like other males.

She didn't know how to act with him. A nervous thought skittered through her mind: If she made him her lover would he protect her? Or would he kill her just the same if she was the rogue? *I'm crazy*, she thought, warding off the idea.

At the park he jumped the curb, and she clutched him despite herself and heard him laugh over the roar of the engine. He cruised down a tarmac path, ignoring the shouts of an elderly man in green work pants, and brought her right into the audience. The crowd parted like the Red Sea. Some people laughed and cheered, others feigned disinterest. If she wanted attention, she had it, but she didn't care. There was only one person she was interested in.

She scanned the crowd. There, close to the makeshift stage, she spotted Quince and Bingo. They had turned like the others to find the source of the noise. Quince raised his arm to wave to her, then lowered it quickly when Bingo elbowed him. Around them were others she knew. Her breath caught in her throat when she spotted Aiden. He was staring right at her, his mouth slightly parted.

She ripped her gaze away and climbed off the bike. *What do I do? What do I do?* Against all common sense, she stepped up on the footrest and pressed her lips to Gabriel's. *Oh, Bloody Moon, I'm an idiot*, she thought. It was meant to be a brief kiss to make Aiden jealous, over before Gabriel realized what was happening. She didn't expect the swiftness with which he encircled her waist with his arm. Suddenly she found herself half across the gas tank and crushed against his chest, her feet off the ground, metal digging into her right knee. His practiced tongue parted her lips while she clung to him to stop herself from falling. She felt the heat of him searing her through his shirt and smelled his musky scent growing rich and suggestive. Then he let her go, and she slid to the ground and staggered backward.

His eyes smoldered beneath half-closed lids. "Don't use me," he growled. Then he revved his engine, echoing the threat. She watched him leave, her face blazing, her breath harsh in her throat. *Damn him,* she cursed silently. He couldn't be controlled. She resisted the urge to swipe at anyone she found looking at her.

I knew Gabriel wouldn't be fooled, she complained to herself as she made her way through the crowd. *So why did I go right ahead and kiss him anyway?* Seeing Aiden must have made her brain soft.

It wasn't hard to charm a young man into making space for her a few yards away from the Amoeba. She saw Aiden glance nervously over. Good, he knew where she was. She smiled to think of how his eyes would keep on creeping back to her no matter how he tried to look away. *I'll have him,* she thought.

Aiden stood. Vivian's heart leaped. He was coming to her. She wouldn't have to patiently seduce.

But he didn't turn her way. Kelly ran through the crowd. She flung herself into his arms, and he hugged her and laughed while she kissed his neck.

A hot sun of rage rose in Vivian's breast.

23

Vivian waited until it was dark to leave. She was damned if Aiden would see her driven away. She watched two bands perform through tear-blurred eyes, but the music was meaningless noise—she never clapped, and she never rose to dance like the others around her—and each peal of laughter that drifted over from the Amoeba made her stomach clench and her shoulders stiffen, until she was almost rigid with anger. She wouldn't look that way or she would shatter, for sure.

"You all right?" the guy beside her asked, obviously longing to comfort her.

"Yeah." The word came out a harsh whisper, and she shook her head when he tried to put his arm around her. He backed off, grabbed a beer from his buddy, and yelled encouragement at the stage, covering rejection with bravado.

Finally the dusk deepened and the bright stage lights came on, blinding the audience to those around them. When everyone stood to cheer the outgoing band, Vivian stood with them and slipped off.

She picked her way through the crowd, between blankets and coolers, over legs and backpacks. She passed couples tangy with sweat and cheap wine, and groups of young men reeking with the burping ripeness of beer. Across the cooling air drifted the smoke of cigarettes and marijuana. She cursed them for their happy oblivion.

She found the river and followed it upstream toward her home. When she was back in her territory, she dove into the tall grass and rolled there, clutching herself as if to crush the pain, but her misery broke loose and she shrieked her curses at the sky. She raged at herself and the boy, and cried hot tears.

"I am beautiful!" she screamed hoarsely. "Why can't he see that?" She ripped at the grass, dug holes in the earth, and flung the soil into the night.

She didn't hear someone approaching.

"Jeez, Viv, could you make a little more noise?"

Vivian went rigid, her hands clutching the front of her shirt. One lengthening nail snicked through the cotton and pricked her chest.

Rafe sauntered around her and bent to peer in her face. "Upset?"

"Fuck you."

"Why don't you take care of him, Viv? He deserves it. You could do that—couldn't you?"

She lunged at Rafe and tried to tear off a piece of his face.

He jumped back, laughing. "Save that for your meat-boy, Viv." Then he was gone.

Vivian curled into a ball to stifle her sobs, ashamed that Rafe had seen her out of control. After a while, even her crying ceased, and she crouched in the prickling grass with her arms tight around her knees, her nose full of the dust of summer hay. Gradually she slid to her side in a crumpled rag-doll heap.

There was rustling in the grass, and this time Vivian recognized the leather and tartness that was Rafe before he reached her. She could feel him standing over her but she ignored him. He nudged her gently with his toe, then slid something long, cold, and smooth into the crook of her arm. She opened her eyes and bared her teeth at him.

"It doesn't solve anything," he said, and she was taken aback by the unaccustomed pity in his eyes. "But it makes you numb for a while." Then he left.

He had given her a bottle. She didn't even bother to read the label, but unscrewed the top and took a swig. She sputtered, losing half her mouthful in a spray. She was prepared for the second mouthful, even though every drop carved a burning path to her gut. The third gulp brought on the beginnings of the promised numbness. *I owe Rafe one,* she thought, and laughed bitterly. She wondered if the whole bottle would wipe out her pain, or would it kill her?

If they find me dead of alcohol poisoning in the morning, that'll serve Aiden right, she thought. *He'll know it's his fault.* She took another swig. *Everything's his fault.* And another swig. *I was okay before he hurt me.* And another swig. *I never had a blackout before. I never woke up with blood all over me before. It's all his fault. I might have done something terrible, and it's . . . all . . . his . . . fault.*

The more she drank, the more reasons she found to hate him.

And then he flings that bitch in my face, she fumed. Kelly had been waiting for this chance all along. *How long did it take her to show up on his doorstep after she found out we'd split?* Vivian wondered. *Not long, I bet. Dammit, if that cow had left him alone, I'd have him back. The scheming, filthy little white-fleshed grub.*

I wanted to love you, she thought miserably as she held the bottle in an embrace.

The liquor didn't burn now, but was warm and comforting; thinking of Kelly and Aiden burned.

I'd like to feel my teeth in her throat, Vivian thought. *I'd like to slit her gullet.* But the image of a yellow police ribbon came to her unbidden, and she shook her head violently. The action left her feeling slightly sick. *No, no,* she thought. *Bad girl. Can't do that, can I?* Then an idea brought a thin smile to her lips, and made the warmth of the liquor burn brighter. *But I could scare her real good.*

"And where might I accomplish this delicious task?" she asked aloud. Her words slurred, and for some stupid reason this made her laugh. "Where, where . . ." She laughed again. "I know where you live, Kelly." She almost sang the words.

She struggled to her feet and tottered a few steps,

and when she remembered the bottle she almost fell over retrieving it.

It took Vivian twenty minutes to lope down deserted, lamplit streets to Kelly's home, and her gait became steadier as she found her rhythm. At the house she looked around to see if anyone watched, then slunk into the shadow of the hedge that bordered the side of the yard.

There was a car in the driveway of the small brick rambler, and all the windows were dark, but the lights on either side of the front door were on. It was way after midnight; was Kelly not home yet?

Vivian opened the bottle and took a drink, then leaped a white picket fence into the backyard. Her landing was more of a stagger. She could taste the liquor when she inhaled, as if she breathed its vapor instead of air.

She peered into three windows before she found the room she wanted—a small bedroom papered with rock band posters. The bed was empty. Vivian growled at the back of her throat, imagining Kelly in another bed—Aiden's. *Gonna wait for you, girl.*

She tried prying open the casement window with her fingers, but it was locked from inside. What now? She wiped the sweat from her brow with a downy forearm.

A quick tour of the yard turned up a shed. The chain holding the door closed snapped like a candy cane. Inside were a lawn mower, gas cans, a bench laden with pots, and garden tools dangling neatly on pegs.

On one of the pegs hung a roll of duct tape. She took that and a trowel and went back to Kelly's window. The air was a soup of moisture and insects. In the distance thunder snarled.

She ripped off lengths of tape with her teeth and plastered them over a windowpane, then hit the mess with the trowel. The tape deadened the noise, and the broken glass peeled away easily. Through the hole, she flicked the lock, turned the handle, and let herself into the cool, dark room.

Vivian carefully closed the bedroom door, drew the curtains, then turned on a lamp beside the bed. She winced at the light. A few seconds passed before she could look around through squinting eyes.

The room was that of a little girl gone bad. Beneath the haphazard pictures full of naked chests, flannel, and tattoos, she could see pink, flowered wallpaper. There was an ink-stained pink ruffle around the dressing table, and a loving mother still made the bed up in pink sheets, although it was probably the daughter who had thrown a black down comforter on top. An old stuffed tiger lolled its head on the pillow.

Great Moon, what am I doing here? Vivian thought. *This is crazy. Kelly didn't do anything I wouldn't do.* Suddenly she yearned for her own room, her own bed. Waiting seemed stupid and useless. *Gotta get out of here,* she decided.

"Here, have a present, Kelly." Vivian smacked the bottle down on the dresser amid jars of makeup, bangles, pens, and tapes. The bottle tipped when she let go, and she grabbed for it, then noticed the chain underneath that had set it off balance. On the end of the chain was a pentagram.

As she picked up the pentagram her nails lengthened to claws and hair grew in a prickling trail down her back. "He gave it to you?" Her words were a whisper of strangled outrage. Was this the same necklace she had thrown back at Aiden? Was he so callous he could turn around and give it to someone else? Or did he give everyone a pentagram? Tears coursed down her cheeks as she bent the charm in half. *I thought I was special.*

She clicked off the light.

"I hate pink," she spat, and pierced a curtain with her claws, shredding it down to the hem. She turned both curtains to ribbons, savoring the sound of tearing and the tingling vibrations in her fingertips.

She went to the closet. The clothes hung in ranks — in front of the door were the black outfits Kelly favored, to either side were cheerful items most likely bought by a worried mother and only worn at family occasions after much pleading. Vivian shredded the black clothes.

She turned to the bed.

Her first swipe at the comforter sent feathers flying. They made her think of killing chickens, and she drooled as her claws swiped faster, faster, until the bed was a pile of down and pink-and-black rags. She lowered herself into this nest and her muzzle grew.

Hello, Little Red Riding Hood, she thought.

She remained in a half-state — part girl, part

212

creature—and her toes curled and uncurled with the pleasure of imagining Kelly's face when she saw what was in her bed. She could be finished and gone before Kelly's screams brought her parents running—or so the alcohol told her. But as the minutes ticked away, the pleasure began to dim, and she turned back to girl. Was Kelly coming home at all?

Vivian retrieved the bottle and gulped from it, her throat now dead to the burn. Her vision was blurred, and shadows dissolved into disconcerting gray tweed. Her head throbbed. She listened for the front door, but heard only snores and the creaks and groans of a nighttime house. She paced unsteadily, but whenever she stopped, the room began to turn, so she kept on moving. Every so often she picked up one of the cassettes from the dresser and unraveled it, strewing tape across the room.

The clock did away with luminous minutes until it was three A.M.

"She's not coming home," Vivian growled. "The bitch is not coming home."

She climbed through the window, scraping her shins, and tumbled onto the grass outside. She struggled to her feet, and somehow made it back over the fence without turning upside down, then set off down the road.

She knew where Kelly was. "I will rip you from his arms," Vivian promised. "I will rip you."

The night contracted to a pinpoint of hate.

24

Vivian woke with a start. She didn't remember coming to bed. She groped for some memory of brushing her teeth or undressing, but nothing came. Carefully she opened her eyes. A pain beat at her head like a mallet in a sock; the other sock covered her tongue. Her whole body ached.

This was too much like another recent morning. Her heart pounded.

Vivian sat up amid her twisted sheets. She was naked. She looked around the room for the clothes she had worn the night before. The back of her desk chair was bare. There were no rumpled piles on the floor. Where were her clothes? She forced down the rising panic.

The early-morning breeze that wafted through the open window was damp but cool. The window screen was ripped across its entire width—enough for a person to climb through, a person without the wits to raise an obstinate frame. There was dirt on the floor.

Vivian looked down at herself. She was streaked

214

with green mud as if she'd been in the river. She snatched up her hands and inspected her nails. They were pink, tipped with white. She exhaled audibly. There was no blood, thank the Moon.

She began to relax. She'd been drunk last night, that was all. So what if she'd stripped off her clothes and run around on all fours for a while? She deserved it. Instinct had probably kicked in and kept her to the woods. Yes, she'd been stupid to go to Kelly's house, but thankfully she'd gotten the hell out of there before anyone discovered her. *I don't think I went to Aiden's*, she thought. Of course she didn't remember how she'd become muddy either.

She swung her legs over the side of the bed and moaned. The sheets were dragged with her. And that's when a hand fell on the floor with a small soft thud.

Vivian froze. The room spun out of focus. The only clear thing, sharp-edged, real beyond real, was a severed hand lying palm up on her bedroom rug. The flesh was pale and slightly puckered, as if it had been in the river with her. There were tooth marks in the palm. At the wrist was a ragged fringe of skin that surrounded a dark crusty core and a bone that protruded white. The bone had been crushed so someone could suck the marrow.

She saw a ring on the middle finger. Choking back the bile, she stuck out a foot and flipped the clammy hand over, then recoiled. The ring was a silver skull. It belonged to the biker who'd come on to her outside Tooley's, the one she'd told Gabriel she'd smack around.

She breathed fast and shallow like an animal in a trap. *I've got to get rid of it,* she thought.

Had anyone seen her? Had she left a trail to her house? She rushed to the window and looked out. A mist rose from the grass, but there was nothing unusual outside.

What if Esmé came in? She ran to the door and locked it. Despite the cool breeze she was bathed in sweat. She had to hide the hand until she could get it out of the house.

She looked around desperately. The wolves painted on the wall seemed to laugh at her. She yanked open the closet door. In a boot? No, she'd never wear them again. She noticed a Timberland shoe box up on the shelf. Perfect. She nudged the top off, retrieved the hand, and, carrying it gingerly by its waxy thumb, reached up and dropped it in. There was a rustle of tissue paper, and for one heart-stopping moment she imagined it writhing in there. She stifled a hysterical giggle and dropped the lid on the box.

Esmé was still in bed; her door was closed. Rudy was out. Vivian showered and dressed as fast as she could; then she shook the hand from the box into a cheap nylon fanny pack, which she strapped on. Her skin crawled as she walked out the kitchen door.

In the thickest part of the undergrowth out back, she sat on her haunches and rubbed garlic and pepper into the hand as if it were a leg of lamb. She hoped the smell would drive away any dog that might try to dig it up. *I can't believe I'm doing this,* she thought. She'd had dreams that seemed more real.

She couldn't seem to make a hole deep enough. *Just a few more inches,* she kept on telling herself. *I can't let anyone discover it.* If Gabriel found out he'd kill her for the safety of the pack, whether or not he wanted her for a mate. She saw in the granite of Gabriel's face swift justice and questions later, no matter what he said about being a good listener and his boasts of muscle to spare for her protection.

Finally she tossed the hand in and scrabbled to fill the hole, her knees bent ready to dive through the scrub if anyone approached, her mouth metallic with fear. She prayed to the Moon that it would stay there undisturbed.

Inside, Esmé was up. She sat at the table drinking a cup of coffee while a news show on the radio droned on quietly. Tomas was with her. They looked like a wet funeral.

"Look who came tapping at my window at dawn," Esmé said, with only a glimmer of her usual sly grin.

Vivian's breath caught in her throat, but nothing in Tomas's expression suggested that their paths had crossed. "What's up?" she asked, knowing already.

Esmé got up for another cup from the cabinet. "Someone found another body. The news said it was mutilated, but they wouldn't say how."

"The police hold that sort of information back," explained Tomas. "That way only the real killer will know the details, and they can weed out cranks who confess for attention."

"Where was it found?" Vivian asked.

"Over by the university," Esmé answered, bringing

Vivian some coffee. "Behind one of the temporary buildings where they're gonna build the new art department."

The street Kelly lived on was only blocks from that side of the campus.

"I know, baby," Esmé comforted, misinterpreting Vivian's pale face. "We all feel the same way."

Tomas reached out and stroked Esmé's hand. She grabbed his fingers and held on. "What must you think of us?" she said. "Honestly, you just happened to come along right when things started to go crazy. We'll get this mess sorted out . . ." She realized she was babbling and shut up.

The sound of the radio seemed to swell to fill the void left by her silence, so no one missed the news bulletin: *"In a bizarre new twist in the latest, so-called 'beast murder,' an inside source reports police have been the recipient of an anonymous phone call claiming the two murders are the work of werewolves. Chief Detective Sirilla refused to comment."* The news reporter had some difficulty concealing his amusement, but regained his awareness of bad taste before he made a joke. *"These are, of course, serious crimes, and police would appreciate any real information that would lead to an arrest."*

Esmé leaned back in her chair and turned off the radio. "Shit, shit, shit."

"But who would know?" Tomas asked. "Who could possibly know?" He was flushed and angry.

Vivian was well aware of who it was. *How could he do that?* she thought in dismay. After all those sweet kisses, how could he think she could kill? She might doubt

218

herself, but she had given him no reason to doubt her. Just because she could change into an animal didn't mean she would behave like a mindless brute. Then she remembered shredding Kelly's clothes. *Sweet Moon,* she thought. *Why wouldn't he think me capable of violence?*

Something else chilled her: The newscaster had said *werewolves.* But newspeople got details wrong all the time, she'd heard. Maybe Aiden had told the police *werewolf,* singular. He couldn't have said *werewolves. What did I tell Aiden when I changed?* she thought. Had she at any time implied that there were more than one of her kind? Had he guessed that her whole family was like her?

"They won't believe the caller," Tomas said. "They'll think he's a nut." He sounded as if he was trying to convince himself as much as Esmé.

"But what if there's one of those vigilante creeps out there?" Esmé asked.

Vivian rose to leave the kitchen, afraid of what was showing on her face. "Bathroom," she mumbled as she went through the door to the dining room.

Aiden wouldn't have expected his phone call to make the news. *He must be wetting his pants right now,* she thought. *He'll know I know who told.* The idea should have cheered her up; instead it depressed her. *I would never hurt you,* she promised silently. *I couldn't hurt you. I love you.* She gazed out the dining room window in time to see two police officers coming up the front path.

25

"Go get Gabriel," Esmé told Vivian.

"No, I'll go," Tomas said, scrambling to his feet and flying through the back door.

"Thanks a lot for your support," Esmé called after him. "Well, answer the door then," she snapped at Vivian in a voice brittle with nerves. "You saw them coming."

Vivian walked briskly to the door before she could change her mind and run off like Tomas.

"We'd like to speak to Vivian Gandillon," said the woman cop, and Vivian's heart flip-flopped.

"That's me," she said. Her words came out in a squeak.

"We'd like to ask you some questions," the woman said.

The blood roared in Vivian's ears like a train. She wanted to slam the door shut, but that wouldn't make them disappear. "You'd better come in," she said.

"What's wrong?" Esmé asked, coming down the hall.

"They want to ask me some questions, Mom," Vivian said. Her voice was high-pitched like a child's.

"About what?"

"Perhaps we could sit down," said the male officer.

Esmé led them into the living room.

Did Aiden tell them about me? Vivian tried to swallow. *Or did I leave a trail?* But if they had followed a trail, how would they know her name?

The police officers took the chairs on either side of the fireplace. Vivian sat on the edge of the couch next to Esmé. She had to force her foot down firmly into the carpet to make her left leg stop trembling.

"Do you know a girl called Kelly Desmond?" the female officer asked.

Vivian's mouth dropped open in surprise.

"Do you, hon?" Esmé prompted when Vivian didn't respond.

"Uh, yes?" Vivian answered, trying to look innocent and puzzled, sure she was failing miserably.

"Were you aware there was a break-in at her house last night?" the woman continued.

"How would I be?" Vivian asked, gaining confidence. This was crazy; there were cops in her living room quizzing her about a break-in she'd committed, but she felt like laughing with relief.

"You're not close then?" the male cop said.

"Hell, no."

"We think that whoever broke into the house had a grudge against Ms. Desmond," said the man.

Then I just gave the wrong answer, Vivian thought. "Why do you say that?" she asked.

"Because her room was vandalized and the rest of the house left untouched," the female officer said.

"Vandalized? How?"

"We're not free to say right now," the woman answered.

Vivian remembered what Tomas had said earlier about the police not revealing details that only the criminal would know. She had to be careful.

"Why do you want to talk to my daughter about this?" demanded Esmé.

"We understand that you might have a reason to be angry at Ms. Desmond," the male officer said to Vivian. "According to Ms. Desmond, you might be jealous because she's going out with your ex-boyfriend."

Sweet Moon, Vivian thought. *I'm not out of trouble yet.* She drew herself up to make a show of indignation. "And she thinks I'd break into her house and trash her room over that?"

"It seems likely to her, yes," answered the man.

"And what about the other girls she's pissed off?" Vivian asked. She could feel the sweat soaking her armpits. "Kelly's not exactly known for her pleasant disposition. Ask anyone."

"Nevertheless," said the policewoman, "we have to ask where you were last night between the hours of midnight and six A.M."

"She was with me."

Vivian's gaze jerked in surprise to the living room door. Gabriel stood there, his hands in his jeans pockets.

Esmé started to speak, but Gabriel cut her off. "I'm sorry, Esmé. We meant to tell you about us at a more convenient time. We spent the night at my apartment."

Esmé rose to the occasion. "Gabriel! I trusted you."

Vivian grabbed at the alibi; what else could she do? "As you can see," she pointed out boldly. "I'm not pining for my ex-boyfriend."

"Can anyone confirm your story?" asked the male officer. Vivian couldn't miss the disapproval in his eyes.

"Ask Bucky Dideron," Gabriel suggested. "He's my downstairs neighbor. He saw us leave early this morning. He complained we'd kept him up half the night."

Vivian blushed furiously. She could imagine how she and Gabriel were supposed to have accomplished that. Apparently the cops could too, because they didn't ask further questions. They took Gabriel's and Bucky's names and addresses, then left after promising they would get back in touch if they had any more questions.

"What the hell is going on?" Esmé asked Vivian when the door closed behind the police.

"Look, I had a few drinks. I made a mistake, okay?" Vivian headed for the kitchen and poured a cup of coffee she didn't want.

Esmé followed her. "That's a helluva mistake."

Vivian turned away, but Esmé walked around her to stay in Vivian's face. "I take it you really were in that girl's house."

Vivian didn't answer.

"Are you crazy?" Esmé screamed. "Don't we have enough problems?"

"Let me speak with Vivian," Gabriel said. Vivian hadn't even noticed him entering the kitchen.

"I'll speak to my own daughter, thank you," Esmé answered. "This is family business."

"When the police are involved, it's pack business," Gabriel said. "Go call Bucky." His eyes glittered as he stared Esmé down without blinking. Vivian wondered how he could stand there so nonchalantly and still look as if he was ready to spring.

"Have it your way," Esmé finally spat, and stormed off.

"You got here fast," Vivian said.

"I was already on my way to see Rudy, as it happens. Tomas almost knocked me off my feet." Vivian noticed that the glitter in his eyes seemed more like humor now. "I didn't know an alibi was needed, but I'm glad to help out."

"Well, you needn't have come up with such a disgusting one." She sat down and tried to ignore him.

"I don't find the idea disgusting," he said. He didn't pretend to hide his smile now, but it was fleeting. "The cops were right, weren't they? You were jealous."

Vivian took a sip of coffee and grimaced. She'd forgotten sugar.

"*Homo sapiens* can be very attractive," he said, sitting at the table with her.

Vivian had expected him to chastise her. She raised her eyebrows in surprise but didn't say a word.

"The need to dominate is bred into us," Gabriel continued, "and they are easy to dominate. It's seductive, this power over them. And they're so fragile, there are those you almost want to protect."

He laughed softly, and Vivian wished she could

laugh too, except she remembered Aiden's shocked white face.

"But they're dangerous," Gabriel said. "They're desperately afraid of things they can't understand, and there's more of them than us. They can't fight us fairly so they gang up on us with fire and blades, or betray us from the shadows with silver bullets.

"Vivian, you can't force him to love you if he's chosen elsewhere. You have to let go. You can't confuse the desire to dominate and protect with love. If you continue this way you'll end up hurting this girl, and the police already have you connected with her. Or worse, you'll give yourself away to the boy—then you'll have to kill him because, I swear to the Moon, he'll try to kill you."

Vivian was amazed to see pain in his eyes and wondered why it was there. Suddenly she wished she could tell him everything because maybe he'd understand. But she couldn't. She'd be crazy to. According to Gabriel's philosophy, she'd already brought doom upon herself by revealing her secret.

But Aiden's sweet and gentle, she thought. *He wouldn't try to kill me. His way of coping is to run away from me.*

"I thought he loved me," was all she could say to Gabriel. "Then he went off with her."

There was tenderness in the curve of Gabriel's lips. "Then let him go, Vivian. He's a fool if he didn't recognize what a fine creature you are." He stoked her cheek and for once Vivian didn't pull away. She needed those words desperately.

Vivian heard the front door rattle open and Rudy's

excited voice. Gabriel's hand dropped to his side, and Vivian felt as if she'd reached for a handhold and clutched at air.

Rudy and Esmé came into the kitchen.

"You've heard the news, right?" said Rudy. "Another one found dead."

"Yeah." Gabriel looked grim again. "If it's all right with you, I'd like to call a meeting here tonight. We have to discuss what to do."

Rudy was quick to agree.

"I'm going back to bed," Vivian said to no one in particular. "I don't feel too good."

"Don't drink if you can't hack it," Esmé said.

Gabriel was kinder. "You'll feel better after some sleep. We'll see you tonight, won't we?"

Vivian nodded mutely. It was in her best interests to know what the pack had planned.

At the meeting, Gabriel paired most of the pack with partners; then he set up patrol routes. "This way we catch the killer in the act," he said, "or maybe stop him from acting at all if he knows about the patrols."

Astrid claimed she was still recovering from her wounds. "I mustn't tax myself," she purred at Gabriel, and touched the black patch she wore over one eye, which made her look like a cartoon villainess; so he assigned her to help Jenny Garnier with the children. Astrid curled her lip, but didn't object.

"That'll scare the little bastards into behaving," Esmé muttered.

"I'll stay at my place and coordinate communications," Gabriel said. He pointed at Gregory and Finn. "You'll be my runners for the first shift and you'll only be out of my sight if something goes down. You'll be second shift," he continued, pointing at Rafe and Ulf. "And I strongly suggest you wait at Aunt Persia's if you don't nap at my place, 'cus if anyone's killed while you're on the loose, you'll get a close-up of my teeth." Vivian was surprised when they didn't argue. Maybe they were enjoying the excitement.

"Willem, you're with Vivian," Gabriel said. "Get to know her again. I think I can trust you to take good care of her."

Vivian noted the look of pride that Willem tried to cover when he saw Finn making kissing noises at him. "I don't need looking after," she protested.

Gabriel's frown turned into a smile just for her. "I'll be the judge of that."

She glared at him.

"Why can't I team with my wife?" complained Rolf Wagner. *He's still not ready for Gabriel as leader,* Vivian thought.

Gabriel explained. "I want the teams made up of people who don't generally hang together. That cuts down on the chances of someone covering for another person. It's not perfect, but it'll give people alibis if something happens."

"It's so wonderful to be trusted," sneered Lucian Dafoe. A few grumbles around the room proved there were some who agreed with him. Aunt Persia banged her cane on the ground for silence. Vivian saw Astrid whisper to Rafe.

"I think you have some other business," reminded Orlando Griffin.

Gabriel raised a hand in acknowledgment. "Yes. It's more important than ever for us to get out of this area now. We've put it off long enough. I don't know how much this police informant knows about us — maybe it was only a lucky guess — but if the police don't do anything, and this person knows who we are, he or she may be crazy enough to come after us alone. Rudy's agent has provided a list of rural properties that fit our needs. I plan to visit them and make a decision soon."

"If we don't find the killer before we move, we might be taking the problem with us," said Bucky in a voice raspier than it used to be. Vivian hadn't seen him since the Ordeal. His throat was knotted with scars where the blond outsider had savaged him. She shivered slightly, remembering the way Bucky had gone crazy at the taste of blood. If she hadn't been so confused about her own involvement with the killings, her money would have been on him. She noted a few others inspecting him warily.

"At least, then, we'd *know* it was one of us," said Magda. Her mouth looked tight, her face pinched. Her sister-in-law, Renata, nodded in support.

Raul put his arm around Renata protectively. "How could this informant know about us? Who would give us away to *them*?"

"Who would hang out with meat-people?" said Astrid, looking at Vivian pointedly.

Vivian's heart skipped a beat.

Esmé leaped to her feet, but Tomas tugged at her arm and she sat down again.

"It's terms like 'meat-people' that foster the attitude that's gotten us into this mess,"someone yelled. Vivian missed who.

Gabriel raised his hands to quiet the swell of voices. "We all have dealings with *Homo sapiens* in our everyday lives," he said. "It would look strange if we didn't mix. Any one of us could have talked. Even you," he said to Astrid.

Astrid snarled at him. The others in the room looked at each other uneasily, suspicion in their eyes.

Having a leader was supposed to bring them together, Vivian thought, but here they were, still in fragments, kept apart by mistrust. *It's my fault, if I'm the killer,* she told herself. *And it's my fault, anyway, because I told Aiden about me, and now he can use that as a weapon against us all.* One way or another she was bringing danger to her people.

The meeting split up, and the first patrols went on their way. Esmé, paired with one of the girls who used to clean at the inn, was on the first shift. So was Tomas; his partner was Bucky. Vivian and Willem weren't to go out until one. Willem said he'd come back later.

Vivian stood outside and exchanged small talk as the pack dispersed.

"Don't see you much lately, Vivian. Come for dinner some night."

"Hey, why don't you run with us sometime?"

"Givin' your mother competition in the looks department nowadays, babe."

"Are you eating all right, darling? You look pale."

She gave meaningless, noncommittal answers, suppressing the urge to embrace each person and beg forgiveness. What if they died because of her?

Finally they were all gone — all except Astrid and Rafe, who leaned against a garden wall across the street and groped at each other shamelessly.

Vivian turned away in disgust and saw someone coming — a male. Had one of the pack forgotten something? She inhaled sharply. It was Peter Quincey. Why was Aiden's best friend walking down her street?

26

Peter Quincey stopped short when he saw her on the path.

"You were looking for me, Quince?" Vivian asked, trying to sound casual. There was no sign of his usual easy grin, and she felt a pang of regret that he could no longer smile at her.

"Yeah. I mean, no," he said. "I was gonna put this note through the door." He held up an envelope in his right hand.

"From Aiden?" Hope fluttered through her like birds' wings.

"Yeah. God knows why." His caustic tone pained her.

He thrust the note at her, and she snatched it away. She tore open the envelope and read greedily. It was an invitation to meet Aiden that night at the rocks down by the river. "Be there at two A.M." he wrote. She would have cheered but for the words at the end: "For the sake of what we used to have, I hope you'll come." *Used to have,* she thought bitterly.

"He can stick his note up his ass," she said, and shoved the letter at Quince's face.

Quince grabbed it in self-defense, tottering back a step, and she was rudely pleased to see him look ungainly. "You know, I liked you at first," he said, "but you're a real two-faced bitch." He crammed the letter into the pocket of his baggy shorts and retreated down the sidewalk.

Vivian yelped a humorless laugh. He was too witless to know the truth of his words.

Across the street Astrid and Rafe now stared her way with mocking leers on their faces. She gave them the finger before she went inside.

In her room, she brooded over the letter. What if he hadn't meant it to sound so final? Perhaps he really wanted to make up. No. She was sure Aiden only wanted to see her so he could repeat that it was all over and demand that she stay away from Kelly. She was damned if she would meet him to be demeaned by that crap. But if that was all he wanted to say, why send Quince with a note? Why meet her at two in the morning in a deserted place?

Then she remembered what Gabriel had said would happen if Aiden knew what she was—"I swear to the Moon, he'll try to kill you." *It's not possible,* she thought. Aiden wasn't capable of murder. Or was he, if he believed it was what he was obliged to do?

I don't want to find out, she thought.

But what if she didn't meet him? Would he stalk her? Would he discover the pack's secret? How long before he persuaded others of the truth? She knew it was possible for others to believe; she'd seen her last home burn.

I'm the weak link, she thought. *I'm a danger to my people. I need to be removed.*

She could run away. But where to? The idea of being alone chilled her. *And what if I continue to kill?* she thought. *Each time I kill I take the risk of being caught. And if I'm caught they might trace my family.*

One thing she was sure of: She couldn't stand the shame of a trial by her own people. She couldn't turn herself in to the pack.

There was only one real answer, of course—to protect her family, her pack.

She would have to kill herself.

The breath seemed to leave her body for a moment. Time stood still. That was the answer. It was so sparkling clear that it hurt like ice water and left her brain cold, numb, and awake.

But how did a werewolf kill herself?

Silver bullets, she thought, and snorted. Sure, those were always lying around the house.

She stood at the window and inhaled the perfume of her last night. *It must be fast,* she thought—she must find a way that left no time to chicken out—and it had to either sever her spine or do so much damage she couldn't use her metamorph powers to heal.

Hanging was an option, but you had to do it right so the fall broke your neck; if not, you just strangled. Strangling was painful and didn't kill. The same applied to jumping from a tall building—you couldn't be sure you would do enough damage to die. She could lie with her head on the railroad tracks, maybe, but only freight trains ran at night, and they moved so slowly she would chicken out for sure.

Finally the perfect, fail-safe solution came to her. There was a can of gasoline for the lawn mower in the garage. There were matches in the kitchen. She thought of the inn going up in flames, her father trapped within. Fire—a family tradition. It seemed so right.

As she went downstairs a flash of fear shot through her, but she smothered it with the certainty of duty. She hadn't died in the fire that had taken her father's life. She should have. This would set things straight.

In the kitchen she scribbled a note. She wanted it clear she was dead, and why. She didn't want Esmé searching uselessly for her, deluded by false hope. The quicker Esmé accepted her daughter's death, the quicker she could get on with her life. This new lover seemed like he might stick around. That would help.

I am the killer. I don't remember doing it but it had to be me. I don't know what made me go crazy. It wasn't your fault. Now I'm killing myself to make you safe. I'm sorry. I love you.

Vivian felt funny writing "I love you"—they didn't talk to each other that way—but this was her last chance. She put the note on the table under Esmé's favorite mug.

Vivian collected the gas and matches and left by the back door. She walked through the woods to the river mechanically, the can banging against her thigh. Twigs snapped, crickets scuttled from her tread, and a night bird gave an occasional soft cry. The noises were crisp but unreal, like the sound track of a movie. She felt as if a stranger stalked through the trees in her body.

She followed the river in the direction of the city. She didn't want to give the police a clue to who she was or where she lived. She didn't stop until she came to a spur of woods that grew far out into the river meadow. Within was a small ruined building, part of some Sanitary Commission station at one time.

She climbed inside the shell of stone and looked around. Beer cans and trash littered the place, and a soiled red baseball cap lay crumpled in a corner. There was an odor of urine. She guessed people would steer clear of this place for a while after tonight. A small grim smile twitched her lips. Maybe they'd even think it haunted.

Get it over with, she told herself, and ignored the cold tingle of dread the words evoked. First she kicked what she could of the trash into a pile in the middle of the room and placed the matches out of the way, on a tumble of bricks, to keep them dry. When she tried to unscrew the cap of the gas can, however, she found she had no strength. *This is stupid, so stupid,* she thought as she groped and strained with trembling hands. She clenched her teeth and forced her fingers to grip. The cap turned with a crunch and an acrid smell laced the night.

Vivian raised the can to douse her front and gasped with the sudden cold. The fumes she inhaled made her

235

sneeze again and again. She wanted to throw the can to the ground and run, but she forced herself to stay. When her eyes cleared she tipped the can over her back and lifted it high to wet her hair. She poured the remainder of the gas into the trash at her feet.

This won't hurt for long, she told herself as she reached for the matches, and hoped like hell she told herself the truth. She thought of a Viking funeral: a dragon ship blazing in glory drifting to sea. It helped a little. "I'm sorry, everyone," she whispered. "But you're better off without me."

The sulfur head crumbled against the strike plate; the match wouldn't light.

"Can't I do anything right?" she cried. She threw the match aside, and fumbled for another with fingers grown thick and useless.

"Vivian!"

She looked up to see a boy and a dog come over the wall.

Not a dog. The shape bubbled and stretched and turned into Willem. "Shit man!" He held his nose.

"Vivian," Ulf cried again. "It wasn't you." His face was streaked with tears.

She stared at him stupidly long enough for Willem to snatch the matches from her.

Gregory stepped over one of the lower walls.

"Is he coming?" Willem asked.

"Yeah," Gregory said.

Then Gabriel was there.

"Oh, baby," Gabriel said gently, wiping the sodden hair back from her face. "You need a bath."

27

Vivian's knees gave way, but Gabriel caught her before she fell and swept her into his arms. "It's all right now, it's all right," he whispered against her bedraggled hair as he carried her down to the river. She crushed herself against his chest to stop the trembling, and when he lowered her gently into the river she was reluctant to let go. But she slid from his grasp to strip off her ruined clothes, then submerged herself in the tepid water.

"What does Ulf mean, it wasn't me?" she asked as she emerged dripping from the river.

Greg handed her his T-shirt. It came to her knees.

"Tell them," Willem ordered, his hand on Ulf's shoulder.

Ulf lowered his eyes and bit his lip. "Astrid came home with a meat-boy tonight," he said in his quiet, high-pitched voice. "Her and Rafe. They thought I was out but I went back for my sleeping bag and some comic books, and got sidetracked reading an old Sandman. Then I heard Mom come home with Rafe making a bunch of noise. I thought they were drunk and I ignored them until I heard a cry. I looked out my door and saw them kill him."

Gabriel cursed, and Ulf backed up the riverbank. "It's okay, little brother," Gabriel said. "I'll not bite."

Oh, sweet Moon, Vivian thought. *I almost killed myself for nothing.*

"They didn't see me," Ulf continued, watching Gabriel warily. "I left while they were rolling him up in the carpet they'd done him on. I climbed out the window and went over to Willem's."

"He wouldn't tell me what was wrong at first," Willem said. "But you know Ulf, it was obvious something was."

"How could I turn in my mother?" Ulf wailed.

Willem put his arm around the smaller boy. "I brought him to you, Vivian. I thought you'd know what to do. But then I found your note."

"He called me," Gabriel continued impatiently. "I left Finn in charge and came with Greg as fast as I could. Willem had already followed your trail. I followed his."

Sweet Moon, did he think her a coward? She couldn't let him think that. "I was doing it for the pack," she said. "To protect them from me."

Gabriel's dark brows knit into a frown. "But why did you think the killer was you?" he asked. He folded his arms and waited for some sense out of her.

It was Rafe who had said she'd been heading for Tooley's that night, and Rafe had given her the booze — Rafe who despised her and now consorted

238

with Astrid, who hated her, too. "Ulf," she said. "Did they say anything about setting me up?"

Ulf swallowed. "No. They just went through his pockets. Mom found some letter on him. When she read it she laughed."

Dread buzzed in Vivian's chest like an evil black fly. "What did it say?" she demanded.

Ulf flinched. "I don't know. But after Rafe read it he said, 'I'd rather be there at two o'clock.'"

"Quince," Vivian squeaked, and covered her mouth.

Gabriel took her arm. "Was he your boyfriend? The one you wanted to make jealous?"

"No. His friend." Tears blinded her. "He brought me a message from Aiden. Astrid and Rafe were across the street when we talked. They must have followed him." Sudden panic gripped Vivian. "What time is it?"

Gregory looked at his watch. "One-forty-five."

"They're going to meet Aiden." She turned to Gabriel. "You've got to stop them. Please. Go after them."

"Where?" he asked.

"The rocks by the river behind my house."

"Greg, get back to my place and tell Finn," Gabriel said. "See how many pack members you can find. Willem, you and Ulf see who's still at Tooley's. We'll need some strong teeth tonight. I'm calling a Judgment." The boys took off.

"Vivian, you get that kid out of there before Astrid shows up. I'll round up whoever's at your house, then I'll be right behind you in time to meet Astrid."

"No," cried Vivian. "I can't go."

239

Gabriel stopped in his tracks. "Why, for the Moon's sake?"

"He's frightened of me," she said. "He won't listen to me."

"You told him," Gabriel said. His tone was resigned, as if he'd already guessed.

She nodded miserably. "But only about me, no one else," she explained in a rush. Sweet Moon, she hadn't signed his death warrant, had she?

Gabriel took a deep breath. "Not good, but not the worst of our problems right now. We can't risk another body showing up in our territory, especially if there are others who know that he was meeting you. Chase him out of there if you have to."

An ache swelled in Vivian's throat. "But what if he's going there to kill me?"

"If you don't, he may be the one to die. Do you want that, Vivian? You wanted him as a mate, remember. We don't abandon our mates."

He abandoned me, she cried inside. But Gabriel was right. She owed Aiden help. His life was in danger because of her.

"Come on," she said. "We're wasting time."

They raced up the river side by side, their backs to the tardy moon, and Vivian wished she could lope on all fours, but if Aiden saw her in fur it would terrify him. When the rocks rose ahead, their paths diverged, and Gabriel sped to her house. It was then she saw two shapes, close to the ground, come coursing down the meadow. Even in moonlight she could tell that one was foxy red.

240

A ripple flowed through her, but she forced her limbs to stay straight, although every molecule screamed that the best way to protect Aiden was to change. The effort gave her cramps, and the sweat of panic broke on her brow. She skidded around the rocks on loose scree. There he was, crouched in the rubble.

Aiden leaped to his feet as she ran toward him, his face etched sharply in the light of the moon.

Vivian reached for him. "We've got to get out of here." He jerked out of her grasp. "Come on," she pleaded. "I can't explain now." A twitch in her back and a stab of nausea made her stagger; maybe she'd have to chase him after all.

"Don't touch me," he cried, and brought up his arms. He aimed a gun at her with both hands like a cop on TV. He would shoot, she knew by the look on his face.

"Oh, Aiden." Her words were a broken sigh.

"I've come to release you from your torment," he said.

28

"I've got a silver bullet," Aiden said, and the gun trembled slightly. "I made it myself with my dad's equipment."

"Out of what, the best knives and forks?" Her derision was hollow. She remembered the silver crucifix in his room, and his father's gun collection.

He looked surprised that she had questioned him. "I made it out of stuff I had, like the necklace you threw back at me."

Blood rushed to Vivian's face; the necklace at Kelly's wasn't hers. But this was worse. He had saved his love gift to kill her with. She shivered. "Only one bullet?" she asked.

"That's for me to know." His dark eyes were glassy with fear in the moonlight.

"Well, you'd better have more," she told him, "because the real killers will be here any second." *Poor Aiden*, she thought. *He hates guns.*

"Stop lying, please," he said, the sadness in his voice

matching the way she felt. "The killer could only be you."

Astrid's shrill laughter pierced the night. "Are you sure?" She walked around the rocks. Horror bloomed in Aiden's eyes as he saw her, half changed, her ears pointed, her breasts emerging from a smooth red pelt. She had abandoned her patch, and a knot of scar tissue marred her face where her right eye had been. Aiden's gun wavered and switched to the new target.

"Can I join the party?" Rafe's voice came from behind Vivian, and she whirled to face him. His hair was a shaggy mane down his naked back, his nails were talons, and his eyes glowed red.

Aiden swung the gun toward Rafe. Panic distorted his face. Vivian backed up until she was at Aiden's side. "Do you believe me now?"

His "yes" came out a squeak, but despite his fear, Aiden stood his ground, slowly moving his gun in an arc between Astrid and Rafe.

"Playing with guns are we?" said Astrid. "You know bullets can't harm us, meat-boy." Either she hadn't heard Aiden say he had a silver bullet or she didn't believe him.

"If you leave now, Vivian, you won't have to see him suffer," Astrid offered.

"*You* get out of here," Vivian growled. "I won't let you hurt him."

Astrid grinned maliciously. "Oh? And it's up to you, is it?"

"Come on, Viv, he's nothing to you," Rafe said. "The stupid little creep was gonna shoot you."

243

"Oh, but he is something to you, isn't he?" said Astrid. "That's why I shall take such pleasure in killing him."

"Try it," Aiden managed to say. He didn't sound convincing.

"If you can't get off two shots fast, don't do it," Vivian whispered.

"He knows who we are now, Vivian. He's got to die," Rafe taunted.

Vivian's talons slid in and out, and her teeth ached with the urge to grow. A tail writhed invisibly in her back like a worm. Couldn't she control herself? Was she truly just an animal? But she dared not change. Aiden was as likely to shoot her as them if she did. *Where the hell is Gabriel?* Vivian thought. She'd have to stall. "Why did you set me up?" she asked.

"Clever Vivian. You figured it out," Astrid answered. "Give the girl a hand, Rafe. Oh, but you already did, didn't you?" She shrieked with laughter.

"It was a joke, Viv," Rafe said. "You were being such a pain, acting like a meat-girl. We would have told you."

Vivian noticed the scornful look Astrid shot Rafe. "Why did you *really* set me up, Astrid?"

"Because I hate you," Astrid spat. "And I think I'll kill you, too. Oh, dear," she continued in a singsong voice. "We came upon her slaughtering the boy and had to stop her. She must have been the rogue."

"And how will you explain the deaths that keep happening after I'm gone?" Vivian said. "You don't think she's going to stop, do you Rafe? She's crazy. Can't you see that?"

"Hey, come on," Rafe said, starting to look worried. "It's a joke, right?"

"You're such a tool, Rafe," Vivian said. That wiped the grin off his face.

"Not satisfied with one lover, are you?" Astrid snarled. "You took Gabriel from me but you want to keep the boy as well."

Her words surprised Rafe. "She didn't take Gabriel from you."

"I could have had him if it wasn't for her."

"But he didn't want you," Rafe said, hurt and rage in his voice. He no longer faced Vivian and Aiden.

"I would have changed his mind," Astrid answered, turning on Rafe.

Vivian couldn't believe her luck.

"But you've got me now. Why should it matter?" Rafe cried.

She had to trust Aiden's common sense or they both would die. "Shoot him. I'll take her." She yanked off her T-shirt and ran.

The change ripped through her. She leaped into the air as a girl but came down creature, and heard a shot and begged it wasn't for her. She slammed into Astrid's chest. Her teeth found Astrid's throat.

Astrid made the full change as they hit the dirt, and she writhed and bucked as she tried to toss Vivian off. Vivian couldn't breathe with Astrid's fur in her nose, but she wouldn't let go. Astrid's back claws scrabbled at Vivian's belly, but Vivian flipped the red wolf onto her side and bore her down. The taste of blood exploded in Vivian's mouth. *Frighten me, would you, bitch?* she raved inside. *Make me think I'm out of control? I'll show you out of control.* She realized the rumbling in her head was the sound of her own growling rage.

Then suddenly she was shaken like a rag and discovered herself in the air. The shock half changed her back to human form.

"The Law is mine to mete out," thundered Gabriel. "But good work," he whispered, setting her on her feet.

"Where the hell were you?" she rasped.

"Removing a carpet from your front porch," he answered.

Astrid's tricks again, she thought, and saw the culprit, now also in semihuman form, restrained by Rudy and Tomas, while she coughed and struggled weakly. Rafe lay in a still heap on the ground. He was in his skin, so probably dead. *Great Moon, the kid can shoot after all,* she thought and shuddered. Her eyes searched out Aiden.

Aiden looked around wildly as, one by one, others of the pack made themselves known and formed a semicircle on the riverbank. Some were in skin and some were in fur, others were in between; eyes blazed red, golden, and green in the light of the sinking moon. Vivian saw Esmé. Orlando Griffin and Persia Devereux were there.

"You have condemned yourself with your own words," said Gabriel to Astrid as he approached her. "You killed humans for the joy of it. You deliberately

246

endangered the pack and tormented one of your own."
He stood in front of her now. "You will always be a
danger to us. We have no prisons, we have no jailors.
This is the only sentence."

He swiftly reached out with both hands and
snapped Astrid's neck. She fell to the ground and
kicked a few times, they lay still.

As Gabriel turned from the corpse Vivian saw pain
in his eyes, not pleasure, and she understood the
burden he took on as leader. But his lips tightened and
determination veiled his sorrow. "This is the Law," he
cried.

"This is the Law," came the shout from all. Those in
fur set up a howl. The others joined in. Ulf was crying
into his fists, and Willem and Finn on four legs nudged
in close to comfort him.

Gabriel called for silence. A full howling wasn't
wise in this place.

Aiden! Vivian realized she had forgotten him. He
crouched on the ground, retching. "It's okay now," she
told him gently. "You can go."

Gabriel came closer, offering his hand. Aiden
flinched and raised his arm. He still held the gun.

"No!" Vivian cried. "He's letting you go." She
stepped in front of Gabriel as the shot exploded. A
force in her chest knocked her backward. A dark
shape flew past her. There were millions of stars in the
sky. Somewhere far off Esmé screamed.

"Stay back. I have him," Gabriel ordered.

She felt hands upon her, but she couldn't see. She

smelled Esmé's Paris perfume, and the powdery scent of old woman was everywhere. Aunt Persia ordered Bucky to run for her bag.

"Look at what you've done," said Gabriel, and her vision cleared as if her eyes craved the sight of him. She saw Aiden over her, Gabriel gripping his arms. Tears ran down Aiden's face.

"You have shot the only one here who cares about you," Gabriel said, and his fangs had grown.

"I'm sorry. I'm so sorry," Aiden whispered. "I didn't mean to hit you. I thought I could kill you when I came here, but when I saw you I knew I couldn't. Now I've done it anyway."

"No one's dead yet, boy," snapped Aunt Persia.

It took all the energy Vivian had to speak. "Let him go," she said.

A flicker of tenderness crossed Gabriel's face. "For you," he answered. "Boy," he said harshly. "There are more of us than you will ever know. If you breathe a word of this, it will get back to me. There is nowhere you will be safe."

Aiden looked around the assembled pack, his eyes stricken and huge. He nodded, unable to talk. His world had changed. Now shadows would always take on threatening shapes. What had she done? Oh, poor, poor boy. She was indeed a monster. She had made him unsafe forever.

"Make a path," Gabriel ordered. He released Aiden's arms.

Aiden took a step, then paused. "Please," he said in a small voice. "Let me know how she is."

248

"If she dies you will know," Gabriel growled.

Aiden took off running.

"Vivian, my darling," said Aunt Persia. "It would help me if you took on one form or the other."

Vivian gathered that inner force she couldn't name and tried the secret squeeze. *Wolf*, she thought, naming her animal shape with its imperfect name, but nausea ripped through her. The thought of her fur form disgusted her. Human then. She tried again, but nothing happened. She tried again and again and again.

I can't change, she thought, her gorge rising. *I can't change.*

She was stuck in between.

SEPTEMBER

Harvest Moon

29

Vivian held a brush in her clawed hand and swept fat strokes across the mural, obliterating the forest and the wolves on her bedroom wall with patchy white paint. *This is no longer mine,* she thought. *It hasn't been mine for a long, long time. It will never be mine again.*

She hadn't been out of the house for more than two and a half weeks, she barely spoke to her family, and whenever Gabriel visited she retreated to her room. Why would he want to see her now?

Aunt Persia had come by twice with herbal potions she had concocted. Nothing worked. "It's up to you now," she had said. In other words, it was useless. Over and over again Vivian had clenched her muscles and willed herself to change one way or the other, but she was like a rusty lock stuck in between—no matter how hard she forced, the key would move neither forward nor back. The full moon had come and gone, and she had stayed the same—immutable, unchanging, frozen.

It's all my fault, she thought as she roughly wiped a

furred arm across her forehead, pushing up the sleeve of her loose silk robe. *I tried to be what I wasn't, and now I can't even be what I should. I'm a freak.*

She splattered the paint in a sudden arc of anger. "A freak! A freak! A freak!" she screamed. And because of her an innocent boy was dead.

The newspapers had already forgotten Peter Quincey, but police cruisers still crawled the neighborhood at triple the usual frequency, concerned civic groups met at the high school, and kids were told to be off the streets by eleven o'clock. No one was sure a detective wouldn't show up on their doorstep. The whole pack was relieved at the news that Gabriel had approved the purchase of a property in Vermont. The parcel included an inn and land right next to the Green Mountain National Forest. They could go back to the family business and be isolated enough to run free. In a week or so Gabriel was going up to sign the papers. They could make plans. They could think of the future.

"The future." Sputum shot between Vivian's fangs and joined the paint on the wall. What future did she have? *I'm not going,* she decided. How long would the pack be kind to her? What would she be but an ugly reminder of their year in the suburbs? And how could she bear to pretend to live a normal life when she could never run with the pack again? She belonged with the freaks in a carnival, but she'd stay here, in this room, hidden.

There was a scratching out back and one of her tufted ears tilted in the direction of the window. *Damn them,* she thought. Willem and the others had spent many a night on the porch roof outside her window. They refused to let her be alone. "We're still the Five, Vivie," Willem had said. "Yeah, you're one of us," Finn had agreed. If the night had been cooler she could have closed the window and ignored them, but she didn't feel like suffocating just to spite them.

She pulled her robe closed and slouched to the window, as erect as her spine would allow. Sure enough Willem, Gregory, and Ulf swarmed onto the roof. Finn dropped from the branches of the oak with a soft thud. Behind them heat lightning flashed in the purple sky, drowning the stars. As usual, the guys were naked and half changed. "It's the latest style," Willem had said when she'd complained. "All the best people are wearing it." Once more she silently thanked the unknown landscaper who had planted trees that sheltered the roof from both sun and prying eyes.

"We've got another one for you," Willem said.

Vivian snorted. They were going through everyone's music collections looking for werewolf songs. To inspire her, Finn said, although she suspected it was for his own amusement. Last night they had sung "Moon over Bourbon Street" by someone called Sting. Their singing was hideous. The night before, while they were performing "Werewolves of London," Esmé had threatened to turn the hose on them, if she could only stop laughing.

Esmé was much too happy nowadays, since Tomas had moved in with them. Vivian had tried to spoil it by pointing out how he had run when the police came calling. Esmé had just giggled. "He's a lover, not a fighter," she said. *My mother should be worried about me, not drooling over a boyfriend,* Vivian thought, forgetting the number of times Esmé had come tapping at her bedroom door only to be shunned.

Gregory announced this evening's selection, "No One Lives Forever," by Oingo Boingo. Vivian rolled her golden eyes and hoped that whoever had donated the CD had been forced to listen to them practice. She turned her back on them, but her rejection didn't make them hesitate.

Even Ulf joined in these serenades, although he talked even less than usual nowadays. Gabriel had taken him in, according to Gregory, who had looked envious as he told her.

"Yeah, calls him little brother," Finn had mocked, but Vivian had seen a rare, fleeting smile on Ulf's face.

"Ass kisser," Gregory had accused affectionately, spitting at Ulf.

Everyone was happy except her.

"Come on, Vivie," Willem called through the window, startling her. "Come for a run in the woods." She hadn't even realized that the song was over.

"No," she answered without turning to face him. "And *you* wouldn't stay out after curfew if you were smart." She heard his sigh.

The boys left the roof quietly.

Downstairs the front door slammed and Esmé's laughter floated up from below. After a brief pause, Vivian heard the cadence of Esmé's steps up the stairs and then the predictable knock at her bedroom door.

"Vivian, honey?" Esmé's voice was tentative. "Haven't you been downstairs today?"

Vivian didn't answer. She felt mean, but she didn't want to talk.

"Vivian!" Esmé's voice was sharp. "Stop being a jerk. So what if you're stuck. Deal with it."

"That's easy for you to say," Vivian shot back.

"Oh, baby." Esmé sounded contrite. "We'll soon be up in Vermont. It'll be better there. You'll be able to get more fresh air."

"Instead of being 'the secret in the upstairs room,' you mean?"

"Oh, have it your own way," Esmé snapped, and Vivian heard her retreat downstairs.

A tapping on her window frame made her start. *What do they want now?* she thought angrily, and turned to tell the boys to get lost.

Gabriel stood outside.

She ran to the window and tried to close it, but with one hand and little effort he stopped her. His eyes were dark stars, his expression unreadable.

"Once upon a time," he said in a voice that was velvet thunder, "I killed the girl I loved."

30

Vivian backed away from the window, afraid to take her eyes from Gabriel's face.

He ripped out what was left of the screen with one fierce yank. "I've never told anyone before, but I've come to tell you." He climbed into her room.

"Say what you came to say," Vivian demanded, her heart pounding. The faster he did the faster he would leave.

Gabriel looked around and stroked his lower lip thoughtfully with his thumb. He sat on her bed. The springs creaked in protest as he propped himself up against her pillows and stretched out his legs. He was too large for her room; his occupation of her bed too intimate. Vivian pulled the neck of her robe closer together.

"When I was first out in the world," he said, "I met a dancer in a bar. She was out of place there—too educated, too sensitive—but she had fallen on hard times. She needed someone to protect her from the guys who came on too strong. I loved to watch her dance. She was lithe and beautiful, but there was something fragile about her because, of course, she couldn't change. Just looking at her made me feel large and powerful. This excited me."

Vivian lowered herself into her desk chair. This story annoyed her.

"I couldn't keep away from the bar," Gabriel said. "The girl became my obsession. I would have done anything for her. I was surprised at how quickly I won her, because I thought she was too good for me. We became lovers and I was the happiest I had ever been. She was gentle and enthusiastic, and I believed I satisfied her, but there was always something missing for me. That feeling tormented me but I couldn't put my finger on the cause."

Vivian remembered how Aiden was always still kissing when she wanted him to bite. "I don't want to hear this," she interrupted, blushing.

Gabriel gave a short, humorless laugh. "No doubt you don't, but you will."

Vivian sighed and shut up.

Gabriel continued. "I found, however, that if I changed only the tiniest bit while we made love I had more pleasure. I thought that perhaps I felt guilty for keeping the truth of what I was from the woman I loved, and that by changing I was being more honest without actually telling her. But it became harder and harder for me not to change all the way when we were in bed together."

Up to now, Gabriel had stared straight at Vivian with a solemn intensity, but now his gaze went beyond her as if looking into the past.

"Then, one night, I went too far and I couldn't turn back." The muscles in his arms tightened and bulged as he clutched the sheets. His voice became harsh. "In the midst of a kiss, she pulled away from me and cried in terror. It was unbearable. I should have understood her fear but logic had fled. Here was my true self and she hated me. I was ashamed to scare her, crushed and angry that she rejected me. I shook her while I still had arms. 'It's only me,' I cried. 'I love you.' But my mouth had lost the shape for speech.

"She screamed and called me a filthy beast. Her words ripped me to the soul. The room flamed red. I hit her."

Gabriel closed his eyes. "One of our own could have taken that blow."

Vivian watched the rise and fall of his chest as he struggled for control. Without realizing what she did, she rose and went to him.

When he opened his eyes and looked up at her, he appeared much younger than he had before. *He's only twenty-four,* Vivian remembered. It was his self-assurance that made him seem much older.

"I didn't mean to kill her," Gabriel said. His voice cracked.

Vivian recalled the fear on Aiden's face, and the despair she'd felt. She sank to the bed beside Gabriel. "I know, I know." She took him into her arms.

If she hadn't jumped out the window, she could have killed Aiden.

Gabriel held on to her, his head on her shoulder. "I fled from that town, and I lived for months like a stray. I was ashamed to take on human form again."

They were quiet for a long time as she stroked his hair. Finally he sighed. "Thank you."

"You could have warned me," she muttered.

"Would you have listened?" he asked.

"No."

Gabriel kissed her neck slowly and deliberately. She jerked away. How could he bear to kiss her when she looked the way she did?

He must have guessed her thoughts. "Vivian, you are beautiful in anything you wear."

She blushed. "Why would we even be attracted to one of them?" she asked.

"Lots of reasons," he said absently as he gazed longingly at her lips. "They look like us, at least what we look like sometimes, and when you're lonely—"

"But they're not like us," Vivian broke in.

"They can't change," Gabriel said, abandoning her lips in favor of her eyes. "But I do believe they have a beast within. In some it's buried so deep they'll never feel it; in others it stirs, and if a person can't give it a safe voice it warps and rots and breaks out in evil ways. They may not be able to change, but they still can be the beast of their own nightmares. It's our blessing that we can exorcise those demons. Sometimes it's our curse."

261

"You've thought about this a lot," Vivian said. She'd taken him for all action, orders, arrogance.

He reached for her hand. This time she didn't pull away.

"But they can't love us," she said. "Not when they know what we are. What's that legend? A werewolf can be killed by a silver bullet fired by someone who loves him. I guess Aiden didn't love me. I didn't die."

Gabriel squeezed her hand. "Silly girl. He didn't love Rafe, and Rafe is sure as hell dead. His aim wasn't as good when he hit you, and we got the bullet out in time before it poisoned you."

"Did you? Then why am I stuck?"

He tugged her to him and caught her in his arms. "You don't understand, do you?"

"Understand what?" she asked, struggling unsuccessfully to get away.

"It's your choice," Gabriel said, nuzzling her ear. "You're doing it to yourself. If you want to, you can make the change. Relax. Let go."

"No, I can't," she said, panic trembling in her voice.

"Yes, you can," he insisted huskily. "And I know how to help you." His lips descended on hers.

She was surprised by the intensity of his kiss. It sent a swift pang through her, and she yielded up her mouth without thinking. He tasted her thoroughly, his tongue caressing hers, demanding that she respond, and she found her hands tangled in his hair, refusing to let him stop, her nose filled with the spicy dark smell of him.

This was the kiss she had craved. The kiss that

Aiden couldn't give her. Gabriel bit her lip, and she gasped and captured his mouth again with her own. He was raw and sharp and rich and throbbing with life. He was sweet blood after a long hunt. How could she have mistaken Aiden's kisses for this? They had been delicious and smooth like the brief comfort of chocolate, but they had never been enough.

Gabriel pulled her over his body to lie on the bed beside him. His kisses pressed her down into the oblivion of the mattress as her hands explored his chest, his shoulders, his face.

"I want to lay my kill at your feet," he said, more groan than words, and held her tight by her hair as he marked her neck with his teeth.

She writhed against him. She wanted to bite him, she wanted to rip the flesh from his back, but most terrible of all, she didn't want him to stop. Her back arched, her body shattered, she howled. Gabriel flung himself away. She struggled in a tangle of sheets and robe, floundering, and fell off the bed on all fours.

She let out a yelp of astonishment, then turned in circles trying to look at herself.

Gabriel sat there laughing. His hair had grown shaggy, the teeth he showed were feral. He smelled wonderful.

"Vivian," he said, a rasp in his deep voice. "When we love someone we want our lover as mate in both our skin and our fur. We couldn't do anything but reveal ourselves to our human choices."

Vivian trembled. What if her change was only one way? The bile of fear rose in her gullet. She had to prove that she was truly unstuck. Screwing her eyes tight, she claimed her human form again—and it was so easy, like breathing. She staggered slightly with the excess effort.

"It was only a matter of time," she said, not wanting him to be right, yet wanting him.

Gabriel smiled at her tenderly. "No. I think that you've just proved that you'll have me."

He reached for her and kissed her again, his claws tracing lines down her back, and her legs turned to liquid, and this time it wasn't from the change.

"Why me?" she asked, holding on to him.

"Because you cared," he whispered. "You cared so much for your people, it broke your heart to see the pack in ruins. You cared so much for your mother, you risked your life for hers. You cared enough to save someone who wanted you dead. And because you walk like a queen. And just because of the beautiful curve of your neck."

Gabriel pulled off his shirt. He tossed it behind him. "Come out with me beneath the stars," he said.

If she left with him now, her world would be changed forever. She would be bound by duty for life, like her father.

Like my father, she thought, then realized, *This is what I owe him. This is how I make it up to him.*

"Don't wag your tail yet, wolfman," she said to cover her fear and desire. "You've bitten off more bunny than you can chew."

She followed him to the window, the blood singing in her veins.

Turn the page for an excerpt from

THE SILVER KISS

AVAILABLE FROM DELACORTE PRESS

Zoë

She paid the cabdriver in front of her house, but when she got to the front door, she couldn't bring herself to fumble the key into the lock. She shoved it back into her jacket pocket. I can't face that silence right now, she thought. It's suffocating.

She went to the park and watched the children play until they were called away to dinner. It was company of sorts, yet undemanding. A few stragglers came back to defy the dusk curfew on the playground, but as the shadows became deeper, and the lights came on, even they were called back to warm beds in houses full of parents, brothers, sisters, and blaring TV sets.

I wish I had a brother or sister, she thought. Someone to take charge. I don't want to *have* to be responsible. I hate doing laundry. I hate having to remind Dad the phone bill's due. Mom always looked after us. The old anger rose. She thumped her knee gently with her fist as if to subdue it. She thought she'd gotten over that. It's not her fault, Zoë told herself. It's stupid to think that. She's not going away on purpose. But Dad's going to be a vegetable. Who's going to look after me?

A cold breeze swept through the park, and clouds blew across the early moon. Zoë pulled her denim jacket closer around her. It was time to get the heavier coats out from the storage closet upstairs. She shivered suddenly, as if ice trickled down her spine.

"It's a beautiful night," came a soft voice beside her.

She turned swiftly, heart pounding. A young man sat

there. The lamplight outlined him against the dark bushes behind like a ring of frost around the moon. He smiled at her as a cat smiles, with secret humor. "You scared me," she whispered fiercely. Who was this person invading her bench?

"I'm sorry," he said, but he didn't look it.

She recognized him then, from last night. As if he saw this he said, "We're even now. You scared me."

"Why should you be scared?" she demanded. "It's you creeping up on people."

"Why should you be?" he asked.

Zoë bristled defensively. "I don't like evasive conversation."

"Do you like any conversation?"

"No. I want to be alone."

"I think you are alone." He reached for her hand. She snatched it away and stood up. How dare he be right, then take advantage of it? He seemed surprised for a second, but then his smile deepened, and a dreamy look was on his face. "Please stay," he said in tones soft as a lullaby. His eyes were huge, dark, and gentle. She hesitated for a moment. He seemed so understanding. Surely she could talk to him. Then her anger surfaced again. The manipulative jerk, she thought.

"I don't know what you're after," she said, "but you can look for it somewhere else." She turned and walked firmly away.

"It strikes me," he called after her in a voice now with

Zoë

an edge to it, "that girls who sit alone in parks at night are the ones after something."

She was so furious, she could have screamed. She almost turned, but no, she thought, that's what he wants. She walked on. Her anger carried her home before she knew it. Strangely, it had made her hungry. She ate better than she had in weeks.

She hesitated once between mouthfuls with a feeling of dread. Was he weird? Would he have hurt her? No. He looked like an angel in a Renaissance painting. Could beauty hurt?

Simon

Simon watched the girl walk away, a cloud of anger around her. He was bemused. She had not responded correctly. He had started to moon-weave, and she had broken it. She had snapped it with anger. He was interested. He followed her.

He slipped gradually into a half state, nearer mist than form. It was easy—like dreaming, really—just let go of body and drift. His consciousness held molecules together with tendrils of thought. He blended with the shadows and became the air. She would never see. He flowed beneath trees, slid along walls, cut corners through dying autumn flowers. He always kept her in sight. She walked fast, shimmering the crisp air with her breath.

They usually came to him when his eyes softened with the moon, when he crushed his voice like velvet. They let him caress them. They tipped their heads back and drowned in the stars, while he stroked exposed throat and wallowed in conquest. Sometimes he let them go and allowed them to think it a dream. He left before they broke the spell of his eyes, to sit blinking and head-shaking in cold predawn wind. Sometimes the dark hunger awoke too strong to hold. He clenched them tight, sank fangs deep into yielding neck, and fed on the thick, hot soup of their life. He was lost in the throbbing ecstasy song of blood pumping, life spurting, until blood, horror, and life ebbed, and he abandoned the limp remnants to seek dark sleep.

He stood at the wooden gate, watching the girl enter a forest-green door with diamond windows. He trembled with desire. Lights came on in the house. He circled it, peering in windows—a peeping Tom, ecstasy denied. He inhaled details from the golden warmth he could never have: an Oriental carpet, an antique armoire, cream kitchen tiles, and a painting of bright, crazed, laughing girls. His eyes narrowed. The girls in the painting looked right at him. Just a painting, he chided, but he felt mocked, and an anger rumbled deep in his throat. The lights downstairs dimmed. A light came on above. She goes to sleep, he thought, and begrudged her rest when he had none.

He paced her garden with slinking gait, examining basement windows and garage doors. He could not enter unless invited, but he liked to know the ways in, and out, if needed. The animal was close to the surface tonight. It reminded him of when he first changed, when he roamed the woods like a beast for what seemed an eternity, mindless from shock. Threads of memory clung to him, though most was a blur. Images sparked bright at times; pictures frozen in the muted green light of the forest—savaged corpses of animals, or a gamekeeper crumpled and drained amid the fallen leaves, his head barely attached to his neck. Simon could not ever control it then, and his attack was fierce, made vicious by his own fear. It took a long time to regain the capacity to think. It took longer to leave the forest. But the forest had never left him. Tonight it echoed in him like owl cries, and pine needles rustling.

He marked his territory like a wolf, and urinated on the back-door steps. It helped a little. I know where you live, he thought.

He walked then. He walked long and far, beating the anger beneath his feet. The quiet, dream-laden suburbs gave way to the street life of the urban fringe. Here the streets pulsed with light from corner bars and pizza palaces, late-night video-game arcades, and record stores that seemed to never close. The hot boys stood on street corners, whispering promises of romance to girls in leather skirts who knew that they were lies. Groups of lonely people huddled together against the dark. He felt a kinship here. He was as separate as they amid the crowd. No one saw him. He was too much like the undernourished,

Simon

ill-clad street waifs of this jangling street to catch an eye.
A group of boys ran laughing down the sidewalk, one
waving a shirt above his head, bare-chest drunk. Girls
paraded bargain-store fashions, their bleached hair and
bedroom eyes hiding the fear that they weren't good enough.
Soon the cold would force them inside, so they clutched at
lost summer.

Simon drifted off the main road to the darker streets. He
hummed pitch perfect a song he had gathered along the
way. It was one of the angry songs he enjoyed. He beat
out its driving rhythm on his thigh as he walked. Occasionally he'd sing a phrase, when he remembered the
words.

He paced the uneven pavement in front of row houses
with peeling paint but well-scrubbed steps. Through one
uncurtained window at a corner house he saw a woman on
a man's lap in a shabby chair. They were laughing at a
game show on TV. He could have stood there unnoticed
for an hour. Suddenly he wanted to smash the window and
scream, "Look at me!" He wanted to be noticed. He
wanted people to see him. It was dangerous, this want. It
was mad. But sometimes he was afraid that he didn't exist.
Now and again someone recognized what he was. They
had to die. If they didn't, well . . . It was foolish not to
think of protecting himself. There was no one who knew
him, no one to say his name.

He turned a corner and startled a dog. They cringed and

growled at each other. The dog's hackles spiked, then it whimpered and ran. Simon walked on and found a weed-choked vacant lot. Its only inhabitant was an abandoned car. He sat on a ruined wall and gazed at the moon.

"Hey, boy!" A call from the high brick wall next door. A leg was flung over, and then a scruffy youth of about sixteen pulled himself astride it.

Boy, Simon thought sarcastically. He smiled in anticipation.

"Yeah, you!" came a deeper voice. Another youth, perhaps a touch older, stepped out from behind the car. He was a big lout in jeans and a flannel shirt like a lumberjack.

A sneering boy in a leather jacket followed him. "This is our lot," he hissed. He carried a half-empty liquor bottle and swayed slightly. His right hand flashed silver. Simon saw he carried a knife. Simon didn't like long pointy things. They made him nervous. He didn't like being nervous.

A scuffling announced the descent of the wall straddler, a thud his landing. The boys spread out and converged on Simon. He rose slowly from his perch, muscles tightened. The boys advanced.

"Where you from?"

"You ain't from here."

"Nobody here knows you."

Simon

"Yeah," spoke the wall climber. "And if nobody knows you, you ain't nobody." He giggled, a high-pitched, nervous sound, and wiped his hands against a ragged Ozzie Osbourne T-shirt.

Nobody. Even this scum called him nobody. Simon stepped toward the danger, into their net. They'd caught shark this time. He smiled.

"Pretty tough, huh?" said the big one mockingly.

The boy with the leather jacket settled his bottle into the crotch of two bricks. "Pretty stupid, you mean." He tossed his knife from hand to hand. "You a retard or somethin'?"

"Yeah. He's too dumb to be scared."

Simon turned his back on the third boy, the one who had said that. He was a sheep. The big one was a bully, but the leather-clad one was trouble. He was crazy. He didn't smoke weed, he smoked green. Simon could smell it on him. It reeked like burning plastic and it killed the brain. It made people think they couldn't die.

"This is our playground, buddy."

"Yeah, wanna play?"

Simon finally spoke. "Is that what you said to your mother last night?"

"Son of a . . ." The big one charged him, swinging meaty fists.

Simon stepped aside, quick as thought. The boy stumbled, looked confused, then turned like an angry bear to attack again. Simon stepped aside once more. His opponent breathed heavily. Simon smiled. Get the biggest one, and the rest often run. But he kept the crazy one in his sight all the same. You didn't know about dusters.

They danced a lopsided waltz on the waste ground, and the big youth's fury grew and grew. Then Simon stood still. The boy grabbed. He expected to miss but, to his surprise, found that the quarry was his. He panted and grinned. He had Simon's arm in a crushing hold, as he prepared a blow. And Simon, who didn't come up to his chin, clutched the boy's belt with his free hand and lifted him into the air. The boy waved his arms like an insect and gurgled with fear. The boy in the jacket spat an oath but was frozen, enthralled. The other boy trembled but couldn't move either. Simon threw his opponent then, an impossible distance. The boy sailed the air for a moment, then crashed in a pile of debris. The sound broke the spell, and Simon heard the third boy run.

But the boy with the knife laughed. He slinked forward, steel flickering in the streetlight. He had seen a fight or two, Simon surmised, but probably won through sheer viciousness, not skill. Best to deal with him as a cat does a rat—no play, snap it fast.

The boy was expecting another dance, not for his victim to walk right up to him. He hesitated a second, confronted with craziness greater than his, then he saw something in

Simon

Simon's eyes that made him lunge. He slashed wildly in fear, but too late. His knife went flying. His arm, captured for a moment, went limp, and searing, and useless. He backed away.

It was Simon's turn to laugh; a sound dark and cursed. The blow he landed snapped the boy back and smashed him against the car. The boy started to slide to the ground, but slim white hands reached for him delicately and slammed him once more against the car. The third blow rendered him unconscious and flooded Simon with the sweet warm pleasure of the kill.

"Call me nobody?" he whispered, and his fangs slid from their sheaths. "Call me nobody?" he screamed as if in pain. He hoisted his victim up and tore the boy's wrist open with a savage scissoring of teeth. He raised the boy's arm and, with the pulsing blood, wrote wavering letters on the dingy primer of the car's roof. I AM.

The dark, raw smell of blood intoxicated. He found himself embracing the boy and pulling the damaged wrist up to his mouth. Faintly, somewhere, he felt disgust. A distant echo cried for him to stop. But the blood call was too strong. He had almost placed a reverent kiss upon the hand when sirens screamed too close.

He pushed the limp body from him, but it seemed to cling. For a moment he felt trapped. Then it slid to the ground. But in the midst of panic a perverse whim took hold. He began to strip the jacket from the huddled form,

𝕾𝖎𝖒𝖔𝖓

struggling with the boy's inert bulk, bloodying the lining, ripping a seam until it pulled free. Black and glittering, he had his prize. He clutched it to him, leaving its owner his life.

Then he was running. He fled past his first assailant, now staring with white-faced rictus fear, though the rubble of lost homes, out into the night, on and on through the streets, until he arrived in the quiet yard of a house with a dark green door.

He wrapped the bloodstained jacket about his shoulders and sank down beneath an azalea bush. He stared at her window until dawn.